CHRISTMAS IN
SANTA ROSA

A STEAMY SECOND CHANCE ROMANCE

LOVE ALONG HWY 30A

MELISSA CHAMBERS

PERRY
EVANS
PRESS

Perry Evans Press

ISBN: 978-1-957434-07-0

Edited by Donna Alward at Words Between Pages
Cover image from depositphotos

ALSO BY MELISSA CHAMBERS

Love Along Hwy 30A Series:

Seaside Sweets: A Steamy Small Town Beach Read

Seacrest Sunsets: A Steamy Opposites-Attract Beach Read

Seagrove Secrets-A Steamy Brother's Best Friend Beach Read

WaterColor Wishes: A Steamy Enemies-to-Lovers Romance

Grayton Beach Dreams: A Steamy May-December Romance

Rosemary Beach Kisses: A Steamy Single Dad Romance

Christmas in Santa Rosa: A Steamy Second Chance Romance

The Destiny Dunes Series:

Down for Her: A Riches-to-Rags Steamy Romance

Up for Seconds: A Second Chance Steamy Romance

Coming Around: A Friends-to-Lovers Steamy Romance

In His Heart: A Harbored Secrets Steamy Romance

Over the Moon: A Forced Proximity Steamy Romance

Under the Stars: An Enemies to Lovers Steamy Romance

Young Adult titles:

The Summer Before Forever (Before Forever #1)

Falling for Forever (Before Forever #2)

Courting Carlyn (Standalone)

Two Boy Summer (Standalone)

For my mother, Janice Marie Dukes, who loved Christmas more than anyone I know.

1

"I want white twinkly lights everywhere," the client said, peering around her living room.

Felicity took notes. "Got it."

The client pointed to the staircase. "And greenery wrapped around the banister. Can you thread lights into the slats as well? I want a lot of lights."

Felicity smiled at the client. "Absolutely. This place will be lit up like Rockefeller Center."

The woman let the tension in her shoulders drop. "This is a very important Christmas. I want it to be perfect."

Raven, owner of the business Felicity was helping out, put her hand on the woman's forearm. "We completely understand. We want this party to be magical."

"Thank you. And you won't come back for the decorations till the new year, correct?"

Felicity and Raven had been planning to reuse decorations for other parties, but they needed to give the client what she wanted. Felicity waited for Raven to respond. This was Raven's business, after all. Felicity was just helping. She was only in Santa Rosa temporarily.

Raven swallowed hard and plastered on a smile. "Absolutely."

"For an additional fee," Felicity tossed in.

"Of course," the client said.

Raven looked relieved. Raven was a wonderful chef and an even better friend, but she was young and not aggressive enough. Felicity would get her there.

"Shall we talk about food?" Raven asked.

"Yes, how about we sit down at the kitchen table for that? I'll get us some coffee," the client said.

"Fantastic," Raven said.

"I'll just do some measurements out here and then head out," Felicity said. "You've got my number if you have any questions at all about the decor."

"Thank you." The woman smiled. "I think I'm in good hands."

"I assure you that you are," Felicity said, and then gave Raven an acknowledging smile.

As they walked off, Felicity glanced around the mostly white, open living room, imagining this beach home decked out with Christmas magic. Felicity wanted her heart to warm at the idea, but Christmas at her house had always been touch and go...par for the course with her family. Some Christmases were big and gaudy and others were nonexistent. It all depended on her father's mood. But none of that mattered. This wasn't for her. This was for the client.

She whipped out her measuring tape and got to work. She was typing the last of the measurements into her phone when a door opened upstairs, and she heard footsteps coming down the stairwell. She looked up to greet the person and let them know why she was in their home, but her throat went dry when she saw who it was.

"Hey, Felicity," came the low drawl of Scott Stover, the man she'd spent one unbelievable weekend with a year ago.

She'd known he was in town. She'd seen him at Ashe's barbecue last week, right before she'd bolted out of there without speaking to him. She'd known she would have to confront him at some point, but she certainly didn't expect to bump into him at a client's home.

She looked down, gathering her thoughts, and then faced him. "This is your house?"

"It's our temporary house."

She nodded, replaying the story Sebastian had given her that night at Ashe's house. He'd bumped into Scott earlier that week. Apparently, Scott's mother had died this past year, and his whole family was in Santa Rosa for their first Christmas without her. "I heard. Your family's here for the Christmas season?"

"That's right," he said, a grin forming on his face.

"Sebastian offered up the info," she was quick to say, realizing he probably thought she was asking about him, "the other night when you showed up at Ashe's house."

"Yeah, about that..." He lifted an eyebrow.

Felicity let out a huff of air and touched her fingertips to her forehead. She stood up tall, looking him in the eye. "I had to go."

"The second you saw me show up?"

"I didn't leave because of you."

He squinted at her. "Are you sure about that? Because the timing seemed pretty spot on."

Felicity sighed. "I'm sorry about your mother. I should've stayed to say that, at least."

He turned contrite. "Thanks. I appreciate that."

"Had she been sick for long?"

"Yeah, for several years. In the end, her passing was a blessing."

Felicity's heart pinged. She pretty much lived for her mother's well-being. She'd stayed in Indy her whole life up until just a few weeks ago to be there for her mother. But once her mother's behavior proved more destructive than Felicity ever imagined, she had to finally get away for own sanity's sake. But she still had to go back. She'd told her mother she'd return by Christmas Day.

"I can't imagine losing my mother. I'm so sorry. Even if it was a blessing in the end. It couldn't have been easy."

He shrugged and looked around the room. "That's why we're all here, together, for the holiday season."

Felicity glanced at the door to the kitchen. "So, Kim is your aunt?"

"Yep. I heard from Shayla that you're working for a catering and event planning company. My aunt seemed to need the help."

Felicity nodded, realizing Shayla had connected Scott with Raven, bypassing her. Shayla knew better than to connect Scott directly with Felicity. Shayla had only asked Felicity a dozen times if she had talked with Scott since that weekend they'd hooked up. She was sure that was Shayla's guilt...her wanting to see Scott happy since she had rejected him that weekend they'd come down for Maya and Bo's wedding. It was a sweet thought, but Felicity was nobody's sloppy seconds. "I'm sure Raven appreciates the business. She's just starting out."

"Shayla said she'd gone to a get together that Raven had catered and the food was really good."

"No doubt. You've chosen wisely." Felicity re-shouldered her purse and made a move toward the door, but Scott stepped in front of her. "You know, after that weekend we spent together, I texted you a couple of times and left you a voicemail."

Felicity closed her eyes, and then opened them, knowing it was time to face the music. "I'm sorry."

"I thought we had a good time."

She shrugged. "We did. I did."

"If you were going to ghost me, why did you give me your phone number?"

She let out an exhaustive sigh. "You know how these things go. It feels good at the time and then you get away and you sober up and you realize nothing's going to come of it."

He lowered his chin. "I know we had some drinks the night of the bachelor and bachelorette party, but we were both stone cold sober the next morning in the shower...and again on the bathroom sink?" He raised his eyebrows, looking at her for confirmation.

Felicity felt the heat rushing to her neck, which was strange, because she never got embarrassed, ever. She pursed her lips and looked him in the eye, which was tougher to do than it should have been. "It was easier to cut ties. I tried the whole long-distance thing with Chase. We both know how that turned out."

"So you have one bad relationship and all the rest of the guys you date have to suffer for it?"

"I wouldn't call what we did dating."

"Yeah, it was a lot hotter than that." He grinned, heating her core.

Felicity glanced at the kitchen door and then down the hallway. "Is anyone else home? Who all is staying here, anyway?"

"There's a bunch of us, but nobody's home except me and my aunt. They're all deep-sea fishing. I had to work."

"Are you still working at the same place?"

"You're avoiding the subject."

"What do you want me to say?"

"I want you to say yes...to a date."

Felicity huffed a laugh. "A date?"

"Why is that such a foreign concept?"

She tossed up her hands. "What is this date going to lead to, Scott? You're only here for a few more weeks. I'm only here till Christmas. And then you'll be back in Nashville and I'll be in Indy."

He stepped toward her, taking her forearm in his hand and brushing his thumb over it, making her stomach sizzle. "I walked into that weekend ready to lay it on the line for one woman, and I walked out completely intrigued by another. I've never had a woman make me feel the way you did."

She cocked her head to the side, needing to find her bravado. "A good blow job will do that."

He shook his head. "Not that. I'm talking about at the wedding, when we danced cheek to cheek...when I put my hand on the small of your back...when you clutched my shoulders. I'm talking about at the airport when you held me so tightly I thought you were gonna break a rib, and then you pulled away and had tears in your eyes."

Felicity swallowed hard, the emotions from that weekend flooding back. A man had not gotten to her like that in a long time. Maybe ever. But she was not going to give in to some one-night-stand from a year ago, no matter how incredible he smelled. His scent took her right back to that dance floor, and those bedsheets.

She put her hand on her hip. "I had allergies."

He gave her his sneaky smile where only one side of his mouth went up with those two asymmetrical dimples softening his face. Between his muscled-up arms and his almost military haircut, he had her tingling all over with his masculinity. A scar crossed his right cheekbone, and she'd wanted desperately to trace it with her finger when she'd laid in bed with him, but they hadn't been able to reach that level of familiarity in their short weekend together. She couldn't understand why Shayla had passed him up. Of course, Felicity had done the same, but she had *reasons*.

The front door opened, and a pack of dark-haired men stumbled in, carrying bags of groceries, coolers, and one holding what could only be a gigantic fish wrapped in white paper.

They were all talking over one another and seemed to think nothing of her standing in their living room. One of them stopped. "Fifteen-pounder, man."

"Nice," Scott said.

The guy looked at Felicity and held out a hand. "I'm number three. Lake."

Felicity was rarely taken off guard, but this man was so full of energy and charm, she stumbled a second. "Number three?"

"In the lineup. Third born." He looked her up and down. "What's your name, gorgeous?" he asked, still holding her hand.

"I'm Felicity."

He smiled even bigger somehow. "It's nice to meet you, Felicity. If you ever get sick of this asshole come find me."

He walked off toward the kitchen along with the others.

She lifted an eyebrow. "Brothers?"

"Cousins."

"That makes more sense. They all look alike, but you just kind of look like them."

He shrugged in concession.

"How many of them are there?" she asked Scott.

"Five."

"Do you have any siblings?"

"Just me. My mom wanted a big family like my aunt's, but apparently having me was a struggle. My mom begged for more kids, all the time, but it never happened."

She looked him up and down, feeling a kindred spirit with him, knowing the struggles that came with having no siblings. People only ever wanted to talk about only children as being selfish and spoiled. She knew another side to that story. "I didn't know you were an only child. I'm one too."

He clucked his tongue against his cheek. "See, these are the kinds of things you can learn about me if you agree to have a date with me. Or, you could stay for dinner. Looks like there's plenty of fish."

That's for damn sure, she thought, considering the gorgeous men who'd just strutted past her. She contemplated it for a moment before making her way toward the door. "Enjoy your evening. It looks like it's going to be an eventful one."

"Usually is with this crew."

She stopped and studied him. He was an only child, but through his cousins, he had what she had always dreamed of—a big, loud family full of love and fun. She could stay, get a glimpse into a different life. But she wasn't ready to deal with the kind of hurt she would have to endure when she had to leave it when this was over.

"Have a good night, Scott."

He just stood there with that crooked smile, as if he had one up on her, leaning against the doorframe as she walked to her car.

2

Scott headed into the kitchen to hear all the stories of the ones that got away. It was the perfect metaphor for his love life. He'd known at the airport when Felicity hugged him extra-long that she never planned to see him again. He still had to give it a shot, but he hadn't counted on a reply, and he hadn't gotten one.

He couldn't be upset with her. It was clear from the start that their weekend together included no strings, but he realized right away that she was like no other woman he'd ever met, and he wanted to know more.

By the time dinner was ready, his cousins had spun tales of sharks, stingrays, and alligators, none of which were remotely true, but still fun nonetheless.

After they ate, a few of them hung out on the back deck watching the quiet surf in the dark December night.

Lake nudged him on the shoulder. "So, stud, who was that vixen in here earlier tonight?"

Aunt Kim sat up, her radar going off. But then again, her radar went off every five minutes. She was unable to stop herself from perking up at a sign of disruption, kind of like the Jack Russell terrier he grew up with. "Vixen? What vixen?"

"He's talking about Felicity," Scott said.

She sat back, looking relieved. "Oh, she's with the caterer for the party. She handles the decorations."

"I think Scott would like to handle a lot more than Christmas lights where she's concerned."

Scott gave Lake a glare.

Aunt Kim drew her eyebrows together. "You're interested in her?"

Scott shrugged.

"If you're not, I'm calling dibs," Lake said.

Scott shot a look at his cousin. "You can't."

"The hell I can't."

"No really, you can't." Scott gave him a significant look. Lake registered what he was saying and appeared to accept his fate. He and his cousins and had one golden rule. No double-dipping between them. They had enough family drama as it was. They didn't need to bring women into the fold.

Lake grinned. "When did that happen?"

Scott glanced over at his aunt who looked back at him with interest. "A while back."

"Like a month ago, a year ago...?"

"Why are you so concerned?" Scott asked.

Lake shrugged. "I'm just curious. Making conversation."

"Sounds like you're being nosy to me," Lake's brother Bennett said as he stood. "You guys can continue with your gossip fest. I'm going to bed."

"I washed that blanket you were using. I thought it had a weird smell. I put a fresh one on your bed. Let me know if you don't like it," Aunt Kim said.

Bennett squeezed her shoulder. "Everything is perfect. You've made sure of it. Love you."

She gave him a distressed smile. "Love you too, sweetie."

Scott stood. "I'm going to walk on the beach."

"Do you need a flashlight?" Kim asked.

"I'm good," Scott said, "What do you need? Another glass of wine?"

She looked at her empty glass longingly.

Scott took it from her. "Stay put. I'll be right back."

Lake followed him into the kitchen. "Seriously, man. You've not left the house since we've been here. When did you find time to meet her and hook up?"

"I never said I hooked up with her this week."

"You knew her before this?"

Scott grabbed a bottle of Chardonnay out of the refrigerator. "I met her last year. I came here for a wedding."

"For that hot girl, Shayla, right? I never thought it was right that you dated the most unbelievable beauty I've ever seen." Lake smiled at Scott.

"Shayla and I never dated. We were just friends."

"So you say."

Scott shoved the corkscrew into the cork. He didn't give any of his cousins the details of his time with Shayla. Scott had helped her through the darkest time of her life. She'd been with the wrong guy. It had gotten uglier than she ever dreamed. But she made it through.

Scott thought he might've been falling for her, but he always knew the timing was terrible. When he showed up to escort her to the wedding, it was clearer than ever that she only saw him as a friend. He'd prepped himself for the disappointment. What he hadn't been ready for was Felicity.

Lake rested against the countertop, leaning in. "How was she?" He waggled his eyebrows.

Scott just gave him a look and went about his business.

"That good, huh?"

"If it wasn't good, do you think I'd have her up in here planning a party with Aunt Kim?"

"So you're going to great lengths to rekindle the flame with this girl."

"I wouldn't say getting Kim help with party planning is great lengths."

"What's your plan?"

"Ask her out on a date," Scott said.

"Did you do that?"

"Maybe."

"Did she agree?"

Scott stuck the cork back into the wine bottle. "She will."

"Ah." He clucked his tongue against his cheek. "Sorry about your rejection."

"Give me a minute. I'm not done here."

Lake grinned. "That's my boy. So she's from here?"

"She's from Indianapolis. She's living here now though, temporarily it sounds like."

Lake gripped the lip of the countertop. "Don't tell me she's the reason we're here? You were hell-bent on coming to this area. Bennett wanted Hilton Head."

"I didn't know she was here. I just liked the area."

"Yeah right. Sounds like a scam to me."

Scott grasped his cousin's shoulder. "More like a Christmas miracle."

Scott headed out to give Kim the wine glass. When he got there, he found her resting her eyes. He sat the wine glass down on the table. "Kim," he said, tapping her on the shoulder.

"What? Oh, sorry. I'm up."

"Why don't you head on to bed."

"No, I'll drink the wine."

"It'll keep till tomorrow."

Lake came up behind him and took the glass. "I'll take care of this for you," he said, taking a drink.

"I want to hear about Felicity," Kim said.

"I'll tell you all about her tomorrow." He helped her up and sent her on her way.

Lake pointed the wine glass at Scott. "You've got three weeks. I suggest you come up with some serious romance."

"I don't know if she'd be into that."

"All girls are into romance."

"I don't know about this one. She's more into...hook ups."

"And that's a problem?"

"I was with this girl one weekend, and I've not been able to shake her in a year's time. I don't want another hook up."

"So you don't even know her. What if she's not all you've built her up to be over the past year?"

Scott had been out of the dating scene so long when Shayla came along, he didn't know the difference between getting close with a woman and feeling passion for her. When Felicity walked into that coffee shop where he was waiting for Shayla to show up with her other guest for the weekend, it was like being jolted with a bolt of electricity.

He'd felt guilty right away, somehow wanting to stay loyal to his feelings for Shayla even though he knew she didn't feel the same about him. Scott had been worried about Shayla. The worst of what had happened to her with her ex had happened because he was jealous of all the time she spent at work with Scott. He'd carried that guilt around with him like a plague. His feelings for Shayla were a complicated knot of him trying to help her and care for her. The second he'd seen her with Chase and how much she clearly meant to him, it was easy to let go.

Scott took the wine from his cousin. "I've spent the last year trying to find the same kind of connection that I had with Felicity. It doesn't exist."

"You've been dating?"

"Every damn weekend."

"Nothing?"

Scott shrugged. "Couple hook ups. But no, nothing."

"What was it like seeing her for the first time down here?"

Scott smiled to himself, thinking about seeing Felicity at that backyard barbecue and how he knew the second he saw her that what he had been feeling was every bit as real as he thought it would be.

He grinned at his cousin. "Fucking euphoric."

Lake rubbed his hands together. "Well then, cuz, let's come up with a plan of action."

3

Felicity thanked the rideshare driver and headed up the walkway to the first stop on the Christmas Sweater Pub Crawl. She found most of her crew around a couple of tables looking festive. Blake and Seanna wore sweatshirts featuring Dasher and Vixen respectively. Maya had chosen a pink sweater with puffy globes acting as snowballs and little silver dangles of icicles. Bo had on a T-shirt that was made to look like a Santa suit. Sebastian wore a green suit with a pattern of Christmas lights all over it—jacket and pants. And Ashe was dressed in a red velvet suit with a jacket hanging down to his calves, with white cotton around the bottom like a rockstar Santa Claus.

Marigold, sporting a green elf dress with a hoop skirt, met Felicity with both fists on her hips. "That is not a hideous Christmas outfit."

Felicity twirled in her glittery silver sweater and black velvet cigarette pants. "It's festive."

"It's supposed to be ugly, not have you looking like you're ready for New Year's Eve."

"Honey, do you not know me by now? I don't do ugly."

Marigold grinned as she brought Felicity in for a hug. "No, my dear, you do not."

"Where's your dashing date?" Felicity asked.

"He and his brother are out of town on business, so Ashe and I are drowning our sorrows together." She slid her arm through Ashe's. Felicity had heard that while Marigold was falling in love with Dane, her friend Ashe had fallen for his twin brother, Ethan. Both relationships had stuck, and both couples were an opposites-attract-fest. Marigold had a free spirit and sense of adventure that Felicity loved, while Dane was the responsible type, and Ashe dressed like a rockstar, sporting daily guyliner, while Ethan was always tailored and dressed to the nines.

Felicity surveyed Marigold and Ashe. "The two of you look like a Christmas freakshow."

"Why, thank you," Ashe said as he brought Felicity in for a hug.

She hugged each friend in turn and then sidled up next to Sebastian. "Where are Meade and Ryder?"

"Ryder's daughter had a thing Meade had to help her with. I think it involved a boy."

"Doesn't it always?"

"Truth," Sebastian said.

Felicity surveyed the room. "Who are we missing?" She was trying not to be obvious, but she had this stupid hope that Scott would be there. His connection to the group was through Shayla, and last Felicity checked, pregnant women did not enjoy barhopping. But somehow, Felicity dumbly wished he would materialize out of thin air.

"Well, Cassidy and Jesse, but we will see them when we get to Jesse's bar."

"Nice."

"And Desiree is on a date. We'll see her somewhere along the way."

"Awesome."

"And, of course, Shayla and Chase."

"Remind me never to get pregnant," Felicity said.

"Noted. I guess that's all of us."

"Mmm."

Sebastian lifted his eyebrows. "Is there someone missing?" He was onto her.

"No. Sounds like the whole crew is either present or accounted for."

Sebastian snapped his fingers. "I know who we're missing."

Felicity gave him a look.

"Tobias, Desiree's fellow. They're on again. That's who she's on a date with." He lightly gripped her forearm. "They're suddenly madly in love."

"Oh yeah? What's the story there?"

"He finally got rid of some baggage that'd been holding him down," Sebastian said, cryptically. Felicity supposed he knew more, but the man was a vault when it came to secret-keeping. It was great if you were the one telling the secret... not so great if you wanted the gossip.

"Nice," Felicity said, glancing around.

"Anyone else you want to know about?"

She pursed her lips, knowing good and well he knew she was wondering about Scott.

"I'm ready when y'all are," came a familiar voice from behind Felicity that had her heart knocking. She turned to find Scott wearing a long sleeve T-shirt that had a snowman on it getting ready to chomp a gingerbread man. He made eye contact with her, giving her a hint of a sneaky smile before Bo pulled him into a conversation with him and Blake.

Felicity narrowed her gaze at Sebastian. "You knew all this time he was here."

Sebastian shrugged. "All you had to do was ask about him."

"How did he get an invite?"

"He got cozy with Bo and Blake at the bachelorette/bachelor night last year. And then after you ran like you were being chased by a grizzly bear at Ashe's house the other night, Scott hung around and solidified his bond with our boys."

"Did one of them ask him to come tonight?"

"Maybe. Maybe I asked him too."

"Sebastian, I told you, nothing can come out of me getting together with him. He lives in Nashville."

"You never know what can happen."

"Come on now, you know as good as I do that I'm down here right now pretending that I don't need to be home protecting my mother. But I'm going to end up back there. The guilt has been eating at me."

"You're not your mother's keeper."

"The hell I'm not."

"Sweetie, I have watched you devote your entire life to that woman ever since we were kids. You would miss monumental rites of passage for a teenager because your dad was in a mood or because your mom was depressed. Are you ever going to live your life for yourself?"

Felicity pursed her lips, letting out a sigh, the weight of her parents' drama bearing down on her shoulders.

"We're not getting any younger," he said with a lift of his eyebrow.

"Let's head out, folks," Ashe said, setting down his glass.

He and Marigold led the way, followed by Seanna and Maya. Blake and Bo flanked Scott, leaving Sebastian and Felicity bringing up the rear.

"Mmm, look at that view," Sebastian said.

"You don't see Blake and Bo as your brothers by now?"

"I was talking about your second chance romance there."

"Nothing is going to happen with him."

"Watch out there, Cindy Lou Who. Santa knows when you're telling a tall tale."

THEY FILED into the Bohemian Guppy and found Jesse Kirby behind the bar slinging drinks. "Merry Christmas Crawl," he bellowed, arms out wide like he was giving everybody a big collective hug. Felicity had rarely seen a man as happy. Cassidy Anderson, who sat at the bar across from him, was rarely found without a satisfied grin on her face as well these days. With Jesse owning a bar in Grayton and Cassidy owning a bakery in Seaside, the two were practically 30A royalty. Everyone gave hugs and Jesse lined up Mistletoe Martinis for all of them.

Felicity watched Scott mingle with her friends, who seemed to be quickly becoming his friends. Every time she looked at him, he seemed to catch her glance.

Marigold, who she had been talking to, excused herself to the ladies, and Scott made his way over. Her stomach went a little fuzzy. Probably just the cocktail.

He clinked his glass to hers. "Merry Christmas Crawl."

"Merry Mistletoe Martini," she said.

"It's not bad, is it?"

"I don't think Jesse can pour a bad cocktail."

He gave her that little sideways grin. "You come here often?"

"That's the best line you've got?"

He smiled down at his drink. "Just trying to figure out where you go since you won't return my texts."

"To be fair, you haven't texted me in over a year."

"True. I don't want to set myself up for failure."

"Ahh," she said. "So you show up where you know I'll be so you can see me in person instead?"

"Are you calling me a stalker?"

"Don't you have twenty or thirty cousins to hang out with?"

"I get tired of looking at their ugly mugs. I'd rather see you."

There went her stomach again. Men did not do this to her. They did not make her all squishy and demure. She was in control around men, always.

She let out a sigh. "Look, we had a fun weekend a year ago. Can we leave it at that?"

"I think you had more than a fun weekend."

Her chest sizzled like she'd been caught in a lie. "How would you know that?"

"That epic airport goodbye."

She rolled her eyes, hoping to avoid her cheeks coloring. "You are never going to let me live that down, are you?"

"Nah."

"I had a good time, okay? But I'm all over the place. You don't want to get involved with me. It won't end well."

"I thought it ended pretty well last time."

"That's why it won't end well now. I liked you. I don't typically like guys," she said, and then took a sip of her cocktail, glancing around, inwardly berating herself for showing her cards.

"When you like someone, isn't that a hint that it might be good to see them again? Or take their texts or phone calls?"

She gave him a lazy stare. "I'm not the girl you're looking for."

"Don't be so sure about that." He tapped his glass to hers again and then walked off. She glanced around, feeling lost. She was supposed to have been the one to walk off first. She was the one in control here, not him. She had to keep reminding herself of that.

4

———

Felicity stood at a bar table, trying to play it cool, but her heel tapped the floor in rapid succession. Who was that girl talking to Scott, and why had she followed them to the last two bars?

Sebastian joined her. "You are wound up tighter than a spool of ribbon."

"No, I'm not," she said, heat rising through her neck. "I'm just enjoying my drink."

"You're about to wear a hole in this nice floor. What is wrong with you?"

She let out an irritated huff. "He makes no sense to me. He pursues me and talks like he wants some grand thing with me, then he spends the last hour talking to this chick. He's full of shit."

"Ms. Haley, I do believe you are rattled. This is a new look for you."

"I am not rattled. I just don't understand this. Even if he only wants a fling for the Christmas holidays while he's here, he's wasting time. I'm a busy woman. I don't get out as much as I used to with my work with Raven's new company and all. I was lucky we didn't have an event tonight."

"So you're ready to go ahead and get on with the affair?"

"No. Of course not. I said I wasn't doing that. I just think he's fickle."

"Or patient."

She wondered if Sebastian was onto something. "Patience, huh?"

"It's a theory."

She peered in Scott's direction. "I'll give him patience."

"Would it be the worst thing in the world to see where something could go with him?"

She gave Sebastian a look. "I've already spent a full weekend with him. I know what he's like."

"He didn't do it for you?"

She let out a sigh. "That's the problem. He did a little too much for me."

He smiled a devilish grin. "You liked him."

"Yes, I liked him," she snapped and then glanced around to make sure nobody was paying too much attention to her. "It took me months to shake him when I got back."

"Why didn't you keep in touch with him then? See where it went? Isn't that what you did with Chase after you spent the week with him down here the summer before last?"

She leaned in close. "This wasn't like it was when I spent the week with Chase. In fact, Chase and I were together way more than Scott and I were, but it still felt like a small step above friends the whole time with Chase, even when I got back home to Indy. That's why I was fine to keep in touch with him. It didn't feel like my heart was breaking with the distance. I would talk to him and have a good time, and then hang up and have my heart to myself again. But I felt an intense connection with Scott."

"Why wouldn't you want to explore that further? Do you know how rare it is to find that kind of connection?"

She pursed her lips at him. "You know I do. But he and I had both just gotten dumped—him by Shayla and me by Chase. Even though Chase and I were just friends, I had come down here expecting to sleep with him for the weekend, wondering if something would register in my brain when I saw him again. I thought maybe I would start down a path to a more intense relationship. Then I showed up and got one whiff of him and Shayla together and knew that thought was down the drain. But Scott came into that situation full-on in love with Shayla. And then he slept with me as a consolation prize. Neither one of us made any bones about that. And it was fine at the time. But I wasn't about to jump into something more than that with him knowing I was just some kind of distraction from her."

"He's had a year and change to get over her at this point."

"I know. But it doesn't alter the fact that I was his distraction. And it also doesn't change that I live in Indy and he lives in Nashville."

"You live here."

"For now. I'm just taking a break. But with every day that I spend away from my mother, I'm in the dark about what's happening to her either at the hands of my wretched father or of that new guy she's moved into the house, and my heart breaks. I need to get back there."

"Why, so you can stand in the middle of flying fists?"

Felicity flinched, stung by Sebastian's words. He typically just nodded and had that pained look on his face like he wanted to help but couldn't.

She gritted her teeth. "I can be there when she asks for me."

He sighed. "I'm sorry. But have you ever thought that by being there for her, you're enabling her?"

She picked up her empty glass slightly, then let it drop back onto the table. "That's what I had to tell myself in order to justify leaving. I put my aunt in charge, but Bev has a low bullshit barometer. She won't help for long."

"And she shouldn't. Your mother has had a lifetime to get away from your father. You've begged her. You've let her move in with you. You've even funded her own apartment for her at times. But she always goes back to him."

Felicity huffed a laugh. "I really thought it was going to be different this time, since he left voluntarily. But she's just repeating the cycle with some other asshole." Pressure built behind her eyes. "I just don't understand it. You know me. I don't put up with jack shit. How is she so weak?"

Sebastian gave her half of a smile. "I think maybe that's why you ended up as strong as you did. You saw the way he treated her and you said no before it could ever happen to you."

Felicity wiped her eyes before tears could fall. "I've got to go."

"I'll drive you home. I've only had a couple of sips of each drink."

"I think you're a bigger enabler than me. You always stay sober so you can drive us all home."

He shrugged. "I'm a caretaker. It's in my nature. Besides, I like to be sober. It's more fun watching the drunk people that way." He patted her on the shoulder. "I'm gonna use the restroom before we head out. I'll be right back."

Felicity glanced around at the others, wondering if she could pull the Irish goodbye. She wasn't in the mood to say goodnight to everyone and have them try to get her to stay. She wanted to go home and crawl into bed with her phone. She caught Seanna's eye, and Seanna perked up and then headed her way.

Felicity pulled herself together. She didn't want anyone asking her what was wrong. She forced a big smile. "What's up, my gorgeous friend?"

"Just basking in the Christmas season and all its glory," Seanna said with a quirk of a smile. She narrowed her gaze at Felicity. "Speaking of which, I hate to ask you, but I'm desperate."

Felicity cocked her head to the side. "Desperate for what?"

"Chase's company is sponsoring a party for this place that supports families in need. I'm organizing it. I need just one more volunteer for the party."

Felicity tossed up her hands. "You know me. I'm a party girl."

Seanna smiled. "Thank you. I didn't ask you at first, because I know you work nights now with the party planning job."

"What night is it?"

"It's Tuesday night. Starts at five o'clock. I can text you the address to the place."

"I'll put on my party shoes."

Seanna winced. "Just making sure you understand these are families in need."

Felicity clucked her tongue against her cheek. "Got it. I'll tone it down. I can handle that, for one night." She lifted an eyebrow.

Seanna squeezed her arm. "Thank you." She looked over Felicity's shoulder. "There's the man of the hour."

Felicity turned to find Scott walking up to the table, causing all kinds of commotion in her belly.

Seanna winked at Scott. "I think my husband has developed a man crush on you. Ever since you've gotten to town, all I've heard from Blake is, 'Scott said this, Scott said that.' Bo Harrison is the same way."

"That's because I'm helping them both with their software at their businesses. They're letting me beta test programs for small businesses that my team has been working on. They're doing me a favor."

"By letting you implement expensive and efficient software for free?" She gave him a skeptical look.

"Hopefully it'll be useful for them."

"No doubt."

Scott fixed his gaze on Felicity and she wiggled in her seat, looking down at her drink.

"Well," Seanna said, glancing between the two of them, "I'm going to go grab my husband before he gets his hands back on Scott again."

Scott nodded, and Seanna headed off, leaving the two of them alone.

"I was just getting ready to leave," Felicity said, before he could say anything else to her.

"That's too bad. I was hoping to get some time with you."

"Yes, you've made that quite obvious as you've spent the evening with sexy elf over there."

The girl eyed Felicity with curious abandon.

"I know her, actually," he said. "We went to high school together."

"Old flame?"

"I guess you could say that. I think I took her to a homecoming dance."

Felicity let her head drop to one side. "You think or you know?"

"Okay then, I know I did."

"She's memorable, huh?"

He smiled. "I think this is you being jealous."

She rolled her eyes. "Please."

"Then why are you so concerned? Are you sorry you didn't talk to me more tonight?"

She gave him a playful shove. "You're the one who blew me off."

"Good to know I got your attention. You ready to go on that date now?"

She shouldered her bag. "I'm ready to go home." She glanced around. "What's happened to Sebastian?"

"He grabbed me on his way out a second ago...asked me if I could take you home."

She blinked and then let her posture sag. "That bastard."

"Come on."

"How much have you had to drink?"

"Not much. I was hoping to be able to give you a ride."

She narrowed her gaze at him. "Would you call yourself a patient man?"

"Absolutely. I've been commended on my patience many times. Once you get to know me better, you'll find that to be the case."

She made him wait a moment, and then said, "Let's go."

"They really do go all out here, don't they?" Scott asked, glancing around at the Christmas bling decorating the streets and the store fronts along the Christmas pub crawl route. While there were plenty of traditional Christmas decorations, beach-themed Christmas embellishments adorned store windows and sidewalks, including a large wooden flamingo sporting a Santa hat cozied up to a seagull with a Mrs. Claus feel to her.

"They certainly do. This is my first Christmas in the area," Felicity said.

"Are you feeling it—the Christmas vibe?"

Felicity shrugged. "Christmas was touch and go when I was growing up. Some years were big deals, some were noneventful."

"Your family isn't big on tradition then, huh?" Scott asked.

"My mom would try, but it never really worked out for us. We found it easier to celebrate with whatever worked in the moment."

Scott wanted to ask more, but by the look of stress on Felicity's face, he got the feeling that it wasn't the right time.

She shook her head quickly, as if dislodging a thought. She turned to him. "What about you? I can imagine your family is full of tradition."

"Sometimes it's more than I can keep up with."

"How so? Too much work? Christmas lights, that kind of thing?"

"My mom always wanted to have these great epic traditions, but it was just the three of us, and my dad wasn't really interested in Christmas because he didn't grow up celebrating it, so a lot of her efforts fell flat."

"You and your dad wouldn't play along?"

"I think Christmas was a sore spot for my dad. As much as my mom loved it, my dad was bitter about it," Scott said.

"Like resentful because he didn't have it as a kid?"

"Possibly. I've thought about it a lot, and I'm thinking, maybe if Christmas was really special after all, that would make him more resentful that he didn't have that as a child. And let's face it, Christmas is best when you're a kid."

She raised her eyebrows in concession. "That's true. Sounds like that left you in the middle of two camps."

He huffed a laugh. "Yeah, definitely. I never really knew who to please—get excited with my mom, or stay grumpy with my dad."

"Is your dad still living?" she asked.

"No, he passed when I was twenty-five."

"I'm so sorry." She grabbed his arm, and at first, he thought she was consoling him, but then he realized she was steadying herself from a crack in the sidewalk.

"Thanks. What about you? Are both of your parents still living?"

"Yep," she said, staying tight-lipped.

"Hot chocolate?" came a woman's voice. Scott turned to find two women with reindeer ears and fuzzy sweaters working a hot drink booth.

He looked at Felicity and she shrugged. "Sure."

They walked over to the booth and Scott pulled out some cash.

"Peppermint, whipped cream, and chocolate sprinkles on both?" the woman asked.

"Why not?" Felicity thanked the women and Scott, then they took their drinks and tapped their cups together.

"I just bought you a drink. This is looking dangerously like a date," Scott said.

Felicity rolled her eyes with a hint of a smile and walked over to the line of Christmas trees all decorated and lit up in different themes—one nautical and embellished with sailor symbols, one tropical with ornaments from different Caribbean islands, and one with Polynesian trimmings, including a grass skirt circled around the bottom of the tree. "These are fun," she said.

"If you had to pick one for your living room, which would it be?"

Felicity took her time, inspecting several of the trees. She walked over to one that was neat and tidy with elegant silver and blue decorations in uniform rows. "This one."

He looked her up and down in her stylish sweater and her chic pants, looking like something that had walked off the pages of a fashion magazine. "I can see that. Fits your style."

"I'd be okay with some of these other trees as well, but I like the order and organization of this one." She looked him up and down. "What about you? Which one would you choose?"

Scott found one that was themed with potbellied Santas

and snowmen playing tennis, grilling hotdogs, and one roller-skating. "I'd go with this one."

She backhanded him, sliding her gaze up to his. "Figures." She had this little way that she puckered her lips with the slightest hint of a smile that was irresistible to him.

"You have a dab of whip cream on your nose," he said.

She stuck her tongue out like she was trying to reach it. He remembered that tongue. He'd had wet dreams about that tongue.

"I don't really, do I?"

"I almost didn't tell you because it's so damned cute."

She gave him a look and then opened up her clutch purse which had a built-in mirror. "Son of a bitch. Look at that. If I touch it with my fingers, they'll get all sticky."

He reached down and kissed the tip of her nose, taking the whipped cream with him.

She looked up at him with wide eyes, which she quickly got under control, morphing back into her unflappable self.

"Couldn't help it," he said.

She lifted one eyebrow and then kept walking. "Try to control yourself, will you?"

He grinned. "Yes ma'am." They walked in silence for a moment, and then he said, "What brought you down here?"

She let out the sigh of a woman who had carried a heavy burden for a long time. "I need a break from my life."

"How long does your break get to last?"

"I'm giving myself till Christmas, then I've got to go back."

"Back to Indianapolis?"

"That's right."

"What waits for you there?" he asked.

She took a couple of steps before answering. "A whole lot of heartache."

"Does this have to do with a guy?"

She huffed a laugh. "Yes, but not what you're thinking."

"What am I thinking?"

She squinted and pointed her cup at him. "You think I'm in some toxic relationship, and you're not completely wrong."

His heart burned for a second. "Okay, how am I right, then?"

She stopped and faced him. "Can we get to the bottom of what you're after here? Is it just another hook up? A holiday romance? A fling? Mind-blowing sex?"

"Do I have to pick just one?"

She dropped the tension in her shoulders. "We had one really great weekend. You were unexpected, and I'm guessing I was to you as well."

"Most definitely." He moved a hair out of her face.

She closed her eyes tightly and then opened them back up. "You got the best of me back then. I was in a great mood that weekend, despite the fact that things weren't going to move forward with Chase. That was just a mild disappointment. Meeting you made me feel redeemed and sexy...like I still had it."

"You damn sure had it, and you still do."

She let her head drop to the side. "Despite my appearance and how hard I try, I'm not that girl I was last year."

His heart pinged as he imagined what could've broken her enchanting spirit. "What happened in your life this past year?"

She looked down at the ground like she was gathering her thoughts. "Have you ever worked a really long time at something and then finally got what you wanted only to find that it was the same ol' crap you always had?"

He just stared at her, trying to figure her out.

"Why don't we just leave the past in the past? You can remember me as that fun-loving girl who got your mind off of a heartbreak."

"What if I want more than I already got?"

"Don't dive down in the muck with me, Scott. It's dirty down here." She tossed her cup in a garbage bin and headed off down the sidewalk.

6

Scott walked into Harrison Pool Supply and let the woman at the register know he was there to see Shayla Harrison...make that O'Neil. Moments later, Shayla appeared at the register, giving Scott a hug. Just like at the barbecue, she hugged him a second longer than she should have. They'd been through a lot together, so her hugs seem to convey something to him—understanding, gratitude, guilt for not loving him the way he thought he loved her? He'd never know.

Part of him wanted to tell her that it hadn't taken him long to get over her because of Felicity, and that she was the one he couldn't seem to shake. But he didn't want to seem like an ass.

Shayla squeezed his biceps. "What a pleasant surprise. Let's talk outside on the bench. It's pretty today."

He followed her out the door and to the bench in front of the store. They sat and faced one another. "I didn't get to talk to you enough at the barbecue. How are you doing?" she asked, her eyebrows arched together.

He knew she meant because of the death of his mother.

But what people didn't understand was that he had grieved his mother long before she died. For years, his mother had gone downhill, and the dementia and hallucinations had completely changed her personality. By the time she died, it was a relief that she was finally out of her pain. People who hadn't experienced the death of a parent in that way didn't understand that the mourning takes place way before the death.

"I'm good. All my cousins are here, if you can believe it."

"All five of them?"

"Yep. First time we've all been together since the funeral. I don't know when was the last time prior to that. It's tough to gather, you know?"

"I'm sure, with that many in the family." She looked at him expectantly. He was the one who had dropped in on her day, so he guessed he should get to the point.

"Thanks for the referral for my aunt—the party planning."

Shayla gave a little smile. "How's that going?"

"I guess they're working on it. My aunt seems happy."

"Have you seen Felicity yet?" Shayla always played it cool, but she had a twinkle in her eye. Ever since Scott had told Shayla he was coming for Christmas, he could sense a bit of matchmaking going on, including Shayla inviting him to the barbecue where she knew Felicity would be.

He lowered his chin. "I had a really good time with her when I was here last fall for Bo and Maya's wedding."

Shayla looked like she was having trouble keeping a smile from coming through. "I remember that, quite well."

"I think she liked me too, but I also think she's got some walls up."

Shayla sank into her seat. "There's a lot going on with

her. I don't think it's my place to tell, but I also hate to see her miss out on a chance to spend some time with you."

"You know about this guy back home?"

Shayla frowned. "No. I don't know of any guy back home. She's not dating anyone, if that's what you're wondering. Or if she is, she hasn't mentioned it to me. But, she's way closer to Chase than she is to me."

"And you're okay with that?"

She let her shoulders sag. "I've got to admit, when she showed up for Bo and Maya's wedding weekend last year, I was gutted. This is a woman who, just months prior, had slept with the man I was in love with, and look at her. She's so glamorous and full of personality. She's basically my polar opposite in every way. But I fell a little in love with her. I knew right off why Chase liked her, because I liked her for all the same reasons. And she was so respectful of Chase and me right away. It's like she knew instantly we were in love, before we even knew, and she backed off immediately."

"But you said they were close. Do they hang out now?"

"When she first got down here a couple of months ago, she declined to come to our gender reveal party. As soon as I heard, I set her straight. She and Chase were good friends. Yes, they had been friends with benefits, but I still didn't want to take that friendship away from either one of them."

"You trust them together?"

"Absolutely. I think female friendships are good for men. A friend of the opposite sex can offer valuable insight. And I also think she could use a good friend right now. Someone she trusts." She smiled at him. "Sound familiar?"

That was why Shayla was okay with Chase and Felicity being close. She saw their relationship like she saw her own with Scott—completely platonic.

He looked down at his hands. "I kind of went dark on

you after that weekend of the wedding, but it wasn't because I didn't want to talk to you. I was trying to give you space... let you enjoy your new life with Chase without a constant reminder of the life you'd been trying so hard to escape."

She took his hand and squeezed it. "You are not a reminder of Brian. When I hear your name or see it on my phone, I have a positive, happy vibe. You helped save my life."

He squirmed in his seat. "It wasn't all that."

"It was all that," she said, her voice breaking. Shayla was not a crier, and he had not meant to have this emotional moment. He had just come to talk about Felicity. He looked her in the eye and could see tears welling. She swallowed, hard. "I know I've said thank you before, but I don't know if you really understand the extent of my gratitude for what you did for me."

"Shayla, you don't have to—"

"You pulled me out of a dark hole." She shook her head, swiping at a tear. "I'll always love you for that."

He brought her in for a hug, and they embraced hard and for a very long time. He knew he needed to let go, but he wanted to allow her to pull away first. This closeness seemed like something she needed.

She squeezed him hard and then pulled away, smiling at him through tears. "I'm so sorry. I don't know where that came from."

"Don't apologize. It's all good." He smiled a genuine smile for her. "I'm really happy for you. I mean that."

"I know you do." She took his hand again, looking down at it as she said, "I want this for you too—love, happiness, contentment...all of it. And if you can have it with Felicity, I think that would be one of the greatest stories ever told."

"I guess I've got to figure out how to chip away at that wall of hers."

"Don't stop trying. I have a really good feeling about this."

He smiled at her. "Wishful thinking."

"You know I'm not one to believe in destiny and fate and all that kind of stuff. But what are the odds that the two of you would be down here together, and at Christmas time? There's always a little magic in the air at Christmas."

He stood. "You better watch out, Shayla O'Neil. You're starting to sound like a hopeless romantic."

She stood. "I've turned into one. It's shameful."

They hugged again, this time just a quick goodbye. I'm going to be in your corner. I may even try to sprinkle some Christmas magic of my own. Maybe hang some mistletoe above the two of you where I can."

"I can probably use all the help I can get."

"Nah, I think you'll do just fine on your own."

7

It took Felicity longer to dress for the Christmas party Chase's company was sponsoring than it did that time she attended the Grammys. She didn't really do *dressed-down*. She had workout clothes, but wearing leggings and a fitted tank to a Christmas party full of families didn't feel appropriate. She didn't really have any in-between clothes, so she settled for a pair of red pants and a black T-shirt with the words *ho ho ho* written across the chest in red sequins. It was festive but casual.

She parked and walked through the gravel lot, feeling the rocks chipping away at the heels of her boots, but they were just boots. There were more where they came from.

She entered through the front door, assaulted by the smell of institution, much like a school or a church. A hand-written sign with an arrow pointed her down a corridor, where she headed, voices in the distance leading the way.

A door was ajar to a room and Felicity pushed it open, finding a party the likes of which she'd never seen in progress. Kids ran around holding toys and pizza boxes. Half-eaten plates of cookies and bowls of candy adorned tables covered in plastic table cloths. Young moms held babies and little children tugged at their shirts. Felicity felt like an asshole for thinking about her scuffed boots.

She spotted Seanna, who was coming toward her with wide eyes. "I'm so glad you made it."

"Am I late? I thought you said five."

"I did. The party started at four. Everyone was pretty much right on time."

"I guess this isn't a fashionably late situation."

Seanna chuckled. "Not at all." She waggled her eyebrows. "It's showtime." She took Felicity by the arm and they walked out into the hallway.

"Who's in the show?"

Seanna led her to another room. "That's what I might have failed to mention." Seanna walked over to a closet where she pulled out an elf suit on a hanger. "Would you mind?"

"You want me to put that on?"

Seanna nodded, looking contrite. "Please?"

Felicity put her hands on her hips. "You could've told me it involved me dressing as an elf."

"I thought it would be better to sort of spring it on you once you saw the situation."

"Fine," Felicity said taking the costume. "What's my role?"

"You're going to be Santa's helper. He's in another room waiting to make his big appearance. These kids are gonna line up to sit on Santa's lap and tell him what they want for Christmas. Another helper will be taking diligent notes, as Chase wants to provide these kids with whatever they want. I tossed in the words *within reason*, but he just shrugged."

"What's my job?"

"I need someone focused on wrangling the whole situation, keeping order through the chaos, making sure all the kids get to be seen for a fair amount of time."

"That sounds easy enough."

Seanna frowned. "I did this party last year and I've got to say, it can be a little challenging."

"How so?"

"These kids don't have a lot, so they may not ask for expensive gaming systems or computers. They may ask for things like their mom and dad to get back together or their uncle to get out of prison. These kids go through a lot on a daily basis. Most of them are just trying to survive."

Felicity swallowed hard and nodded, her privilege weighing heavy on her shoulders.

Seanna squeezed her arm. "It's fine. I just mainly want you to look out for Santa. He needs to take as much time as is necessary with these kids, but he's also going to be at a loss for words at times."

Felicity nodded. "Got it."

Seanna smiled. "Thank you very much. I wouldn't have asked you if I didn't think you could handle it."

"Of course. I'm on it." Seanna started to walk out, and Felicity said her name, causing her to turn around, eyebrows raised. "Why did you ask me to do this job?"

Seanna winced. "Truth?"

"Yes?" Felicity said in the form of a question, not sure if she wanted to hear the truth.

"The elf costume is tiny. You're the only one of all of us I thought could fit into it." Seanna pointed at her own abundant chest and then walked out.

Felicity let out a hard breath and then got undressed. She was adjusting her bra when the door opened. Felicity turned, expecting to find Seanna, but a shot of heat went straight to her core when she made out Scott standing in the doorway. His eyes were wide and he just stood there with his mouth hanging open, looking her up and down.

She turned to face him, putting her hands on her hips. "Can I help you?"

"I think I'm supposed to be changing in here." He pointed at the closet but still didn't take his eyes off of her. "Have you seen a Santa suit around here?"

"You could look for one yourself."

"Actually, I'd rather not," he said, his eyes glued to her.

She couldn't help but smile. "Close the door before one of those twelve-year-old boys makes their way down the hall and I'm kicked out of here."

Scott walked all the way into the room, closing the door behind him.

Felicity took the plastic off of the hanger. "So, you're going to be Santa?"

"Are you gonna be my Mrs. Claus?"

"No, but I am going to be your elf." She gauged the outfit, which was definitely a size or two smaller than she was.

Scott walked over to the closet. "No Santa suit in here."

"Then I'm guessing you're in the wrong room. I doubt Seanna would've sent you in here knowing I was changing in here." She thought about that. "Well, maybe not."

"I guess I'll look next door then."

A knock sounded on the door. "Felicity? Is Scott in here?"

Felicity smiled at Scott. "Looks like she would have after all."

Seanna opened the door, holding a Santa suit. "Scott, I said the room right across the hall."

"From which door? There's a room right across the hall from each."

Seanna let out a sigh. "Sorry. But I guess it's not really anything you haven't seen before, right?" Seanna smiled at Felicity.

Felicity lowered her chin at her friend, wondering what exactly she was up to.

Seanna handed Scott the suit. "When you're both done, text me, and I'll come get you." She scooted out of the room.

Felicity stepped into the dress. "I'm going to need some help with the zipper, if you don't mind."

"If I must." Scott walked over to her and she turned around, pulling her hair over one shoulder. She closed her eyes as she felt him touching the dress and slowly zipping the zipper up her back. When he finished, she turned around to face him, letting his scent seep into her soul, the memories of that weekend last year rushing in—their bodies tangled together in the bed, his mouth on her neck.

Neither one of them stepped away. "Thank you," she said, holding his gaze.

"Not a problem."

Neither one moved. "You know there're kids waiting out there, don't you?" she asked.

"Anticipation is half the fun."

She shook her head, unable to keep from smiling. "You're really not gonna let this go, are you?"

"Why would I do that?"

"We've already had our fun once. What if it's not all we remember?"

"Would you like to know what I remember?"

She shrugged, her chest sizzling.

"I remember the moment I saw you for the first time when you walked into that Starbucks. I thought you were a movie star or something. You were so out of place among all those everyday Joes in their flipflops and their tank tops. I was captivated by the most intriguing woman I'd ever laid my eyes on. And then I realized I was going to be spending a whole weekend with you, and I couldn't believe my luck."

She pursed her lips at him. "You were there for another woman."

"Only as a friend."

"But you wanted more from her."

He ran his knuckle down her jawline, and she had to hold herself steady. "When I saw you, it was like someone tossed a bucket of cold water on my face. Everything changed for me at that moment."

She let out a hard sigh. "There're a million pretty girls out there. I don't think I'm that special."

He shook his head. "It's not just the way you look. It's the way you carry yourself. It's how you walk into a room like you can have anything you want. It's the way you make me feel like I'm the luckiest damn bastard on the planet for just getting to be around you."

She stepped away, putting her fingers to her forehead, feeling rattled, which was a new concept for her, and one she only seemed to experience around him. "These are good thoughts, Scott, but you were in love with Shayla. Don't feed me this bullshit."

He stepped back in front of her, taking her by the shoulders. "I wasn't in love with her. I might've thought I was at the time. But I was just helping her. I felt guilty...like it was my fault that she was in the situation she was in. I felt responsible."

Felicity blinked, realizing she was missing a big piece of the story when it came to Shayla, her toxic ex, and Scott's involvement.

He closed his eyes and shook his head. "We've got a room full of kids to entertain, but right now, I need you to know one thing. You were not my second choice that week-end." He walked away toward the closet.

She turned her back to him, her whole body quivering. "I'm just gonna wait outside," she said, then hustled out the door. She closed it behind her and then shut her eyes, vowing not to let him seep further into her soul.

8

As Scott tightened the belt on his Santa suit, he was hoping he hadn't gone too far too soon with Felicity. He did not want to screw this up.

He'd spent the last year thinking about her. Every date he had, good or bad, when he crawled in bed at night, all he could think of was that weekend.

He'd thought he could shake her by now, but she had dug deep into his heart, and she wasn't leaving anytime soon. He'd also thought she was probably well over him by now, but he could tell by her reactions to him that he had a shot. He just had to have perfect aim.

He stepped outside the room and found Felicity and Seanna in conversation, waiting for him. Seanna smiled at him. "Now there's a Santa Claus." She looked between him and Felicity. "You guys look fantastic. Scooch together. I need a pic."

He stood beside Felicity, and Seanna said, "Get closer." Felicity rolled her eyes but put her arm around Scott, and he did the same. Her hair smelled like almonds and cherries and made him want to do things to her that weren't nearly as sweet as that scent.

Seanna looked at her phone. "Perfect. Let's make our entrance."

They headed that way, and Seanna turned to them before opening the door. "It might be a little intense at first. Are you buckled up?"

Scott patted his stomach where his belt was. "I'm all set."

When the door opened, what happened next threw Scott for loops he never knew existed. A horde of kids ran toward him, tackling him, pulling him every which way. He got no help from their moms or from Felicity or Seanna, at least not until the kids had a good long while to touch him and pummel him with questions. Was he the real Santa? Were his reindeer outside? Did he know the Easter bunny?

Seanna finally stepped in. "All right, everybody needs to give Santa some space so he can get over to his chair." She nodded at Felicity, and Felicity did that trick with her fingers in her mouth, and a whistle sounded so loudly people probably heard it in Tampa.

"All right. Listen up. I'm Ellie, Santa's special elf here from the North Pole, and I'm watching all of you." She put two fingers to her eyes and then out in front of her as she scoured the room full of kids. They all got quiet, some of them giggling, others taking her dead seriously. "If you want Santa to visit on Christmas Eve, you will behave for me. I am taking notes right up here," she said as she tapped the top of her head. "I know all of your names and where all of you live. You do not want to test me on this." This seemed to get even the giggling ones in line.

"We're going to line up in an orderly fashion. Everyone will get to see Santa Claus. Do not fret. You will have your turn and you will get the same amount of time as everyone else does. I am making sure of it."

A little girl tugged at her skirt. "Are you magical?"

"You better believe it." She scooted the little girl back into line and then went down the rest of the line getting everyone in a straight and perfect order as Scott settled into the throne.

Felicity stood next to him. "Have you done this before?" he asked.

"Yeah, it's my Christmas break job," she said, giving him a look.

She ushered the first kid over to Scott, and the kid promptly plopped down in his lap. "What do you want for Christmas, young man?" Scott asked him.

The kid narrowed his gaze at him. "Are you going to write this down?"

Felicity glanced around. "Someone's supposed to be writing all this stuff down."

"I'm coming," shouted their blond friend, Marigold. From what little time Scott spent with her on the pub crawl, he could tell she was a lot of fun.

She pulled out her phone. "I'm ready."

The kid rattled off a very specific list that sounded more like a Target run than a Christmas list as he asked for size five sneakers, a pack of no-show white socks, and a tub of trail mix. Scott glanced at Marigold who was nodding as her thumbs furiously typed into the phone. She wasn't missing a word. "Got it. And what was your name?"

He gave Felicity a suspicious look. "I thought she knew all our names."

"She might but I don't," Marigold said. He spelled it for her and she thumbed it in. He made her repeat it back to him. This kid was no dummy.

Seanna had warned him that the kids might ask for things that Chase would never be able to deliver upon, but they'd been lucky so far. A few kids asked for things like basketball hoops and swings, like at the park. But many asked for simple things like crayons and toy cars, and one for flour and sugar so he could make cookies.

A boy stepped up, staring at Scott with a narrowed gaze. "Are you really Santa?" he asked.

At first, Scott thought he was a little kid, but upon second look, Scott realized he was just short for his age. He was more at that age where he was starting to understand that it was all smoke and mirrors.

"What do you think?" Scott asked.

"I'm not sure," the kid said, gauging Scott up and down.

"Come here," Scott said and the kid came closer. "You don't have to sit on my lap. But why don't you just tell me what you want. This one back here is writing it all down. You never know."

"I don't think you can give me what I want."

Scott glanced at the woman who he assumed was the kid's mother, and she smiled with a little shake of her head.

Scott dropped the tension in his shoulders, knowing this was going to be a more difficult one. "I might not be able to."

"I thought Santa granted all wishes."

Scott was not a *kid* guy. He didn't have any nieces or nephews. He was never around children. He didn't think Felicity was, either. He knew she was an only child and didn't have any kids of her own. And no one in this group of hers had any kids. Still, he looked to her for guidance.

She walked over. "What's the problem?" She crossed her arms over her chest. She was a no-nonsense elf.

"How do I know he's real?" the kid asked.

"He's sitting here in front of you, isn't he?"

"You know what I mean. For all I know he's just some dude spewing a bunch of lies."

She let out a hard breath. "There's one in every bunch, isn't there?" she said, kneeling on the ground so she could get closer to his eye level. "What does it hurt to believe?"

"I don't wanna be made out to be a fool."

"Look at me. I'm dressed like an elf. If there's any fool in this room, it's me."

"So, you're not a real elf?"

"Of course I'm not a real elf. Elves don't exist. Don't tell the rest of them." She nodded at the long line of kids.

"Is he real?" he asked, pointing to Scott.

"I think you know the answer. But I'll say this, if you never admit that you don't believe in Santa, he'll keep coming."

He considered this. "I guess that's true."

"Now, who believes?"

He grinned at her and then turned toward Scott, holding his arms out wide. "Santa, my man."

AFTER ALL THE kids had been seen, Seanna told Scott and Felicity that they both needed to leave the party in their costumes. She didn't want any of the little kids to see them dressed in regular clothes.

As they were in the other room getting their stuff, Scott said, "I hope you drove. I rode with Blake. He's nowhere to be found."

Felicity huffed a laugh. "I doubt that's a coincidence."

"What's that supposed to mean?"

"It means I think Seanna's been up to something. Did she mention to you that I was going to be your elf?"

"No, that was just a pleasant surprise when I found you in here. I suppose she didn't tell you I was going to be your Santa?"

"You suppose right."

They headed out to Felicity's car, and once they got on the road, she asked, "What did you think?"

"I thought it was a little fun and a little heartbreaking."

"Sounds accurate. What about that one kid who wanted his mom to be able to quit one of her jobs for Christmas? I wanted to cry right there on the spot."

He shifted his gaze to her. "You don't strike me as someone who cries often."

"I didn't used to. I've been emotional lately, though."

"Why is that?"

"Freaking hormones or something. Who knows?" She rested her elbow on the door panel and drove one-handed.

"You're looking good in that elf costume," he said.

She slid her gaze toward him with a sneaky grin. "Have you not figured out by now I can pull off anything?"

His chest burned with his attraction to her, not just her looks, but her charm. "I have figured that out. I've never seen you look bad."

"Stick around."

"I'm serious. I remember when we woke up on Saturday morning of the wedding weekend. We'd had a pretty heavy night. Your makeup was all smeared and your hair was tangled, but I still thought you looked out of this world."

She chuckled. "You were just horny."

"True, but you still looked good. You looked even better in the shower."

She adjusted herself in her seat, and he knew he was on the right track.

"You wore those thick glasses when you were looking at

your phone. You had no makeup on, and your hair was wet. You still looked like you belonged on a runway."

She let a huff of air out of her nose. "It's getting deep in here."

"I'm not bullshitting you. You're really beautiful."

She rolled her eyes and cut her gaze at him. "Is this where I'm supposed to tell you how handsome you are? Talk about your six-pack of abs and that little dimple on your chin?"

"What little dimple?" he asked, touching his chin.

She shook her head, but she was trying to hide a smile.

"Have a drink with me," he said.

She looked between the two of them. "Dressed like this?"

"Of course. Who wouldn't want to serve Santa and his elf?"

"Where?"

"Somewhere close to home, so we can stumble home if we need to."

She cut a glance at him. "I thought you said *a* drink."

"You may end up having a good time and want two or three."

"Whose home are we stumbling to?"

"Probably not mine unless you want to weed through my cousins to get to my room."

"I don't know, your cousins are pretty hot," she said, waggling her eyebrows.

"You can't go there."

"Says who?"

"Says our golden rule. Nobody sleeps with anybody's girl. I already called dibs on you."

She looked over at him with her eyebrows drawn

together, a curious smile poking through. "Dibs, huh? Was one of them interested?"

"Don't you worry about that."

She smiled. "It was that hot one, wasn't it?"

He rolled his eyes. "Lake isn't hot."

"The hell he's not."

"Enough about my cousins."

She poked him. "Are you jealous?"

"You're damn right I'm jealous."

She shook her head. "I can't figure you out."

"What's to figure out?"

"What you're after."

"I'm after you. I thought I made that clear."

She slid her gaze to him and then put it back on the road. "I know what you say, but I don't really get it. You've already slept with me. Aren't you ready to move on to the next?"

"I tried that. It didn't take."

"Oh really?"

"Yeah. I dated all kinds of women this last year. You wouldn't believe how much money I spent."

"How did that work out for you?"

"I'm not with anyone, am I?"

"I don't know that. For all I know you've got a girl back home waiting for you after Christmas."

"I don't."

"Oh, come on now. There's someone. Tell me about her."

"Well, she's kind, and everyone loves her. She's the life of the party. Never met a stranger. Really knows how to put people at ease."

"Oh yeah?" she asked, playing along.

"She works in the party planning industry, but it's just temporary. She's pretty tight-lipped about what she does for a living. I've never really gotten that out of her. But I get the feeling that's insignificant anyway. She has other passions in life that are more interesting. I just need to get her to tell me more about those."

"Mmm," she uttered, seeming to like this exercise.

"She's smoking hot. She's got this confidence that's such a turn on. I can't stop thinking about her. I haven't been able to stop thinking about her since the day I met her."

"Sounds like you don't have much of a life."

"That may be true. But all I know is I've probably dated twelve or fifteen girls since her, and not one holds a candle to her. Not even close."

She adjusted her grip on the wheel, eyes intent on the road. He went silent, wanting to let that sink in for her. He needed her to know he wasn't messing around. He wasn't sure how long it would take or what he needed to say to make her understand. He just had to find the right balance.

9

A s they settled in at a bar table, Scott said, "This is close to your home?"

She gave him a knowing look. "You're not gonna find out, so let's just get that off the table right now."

"Fair enough. You don't have to tell me where you live. I'll find out soon enough."

"How are you going to do that? Ask one of my friends? That's not fair."

"I'm not gonna ask anyone. You're going to take me there."

She huffed out a laugh. "I am?"

"Yeah, you definitely are." He waved a server over. "Hi there. I would like your finest IPA, please, on tap." He motioned toward Felicity.

She stared him down for a second and then looked at the server. "I'll have a light beer on tap, please."

"Coming up."

The server walked away, and Scott turned to her. "You drink beer?"

"Why is that so shocking?"

"I don't know, you just seem above it or something."

"See, you don't know me nearly as well as you think you do."

"That's the problem. I know I don't know you well. I want to get to know you."

"No, you don't."

"Why would you say that?" he asked.

"Because right now, you've got me idealized. We had one really good weekend together. And you've spent the last year glorifying that one weekend."

"Tell me it wasn't as amazing as I'm remembering."

She scratched her eyebrow, feeling herself waver. "It was good. I'm not going to lie. But it was a finite moment in time. We both knew it could only last that couple of days. We knew it had an ending, so it opened doors for lost inhibitions and allowed feelings to percolate untethered."

"Is that such a terrible thing?"

"It's not reality. You only got me for two days. You think I'm the life of the party, but what you don't know is that I can socialize nonstop for a full weekend, but then I pretty much need the next five days to recover from being *on*. You say I've never met a stranger, but I'm skeptical of people. I always think the worst of them until they prove me wrong. And you call me kind, but I can be unkind, especially when things in my life aren't going great. I can snap at people, especially people close to me, and I hate that I do that." What she hated was that she could see her father in her during those times, and she was powerless to stop it.

"You're a real person with flaws, huh? I had no idea."

She pursed her lips at him and then tapped her fingernails on the table. "Your turn."

"You want my flaws?"

"I think that might be a good place to start."

He exhaled a deep breath and sat back in his seat. "I guess you could say that a flaw I have is that I get hyper-focused on certain things and I lose focus on what's important, or at least that's what my ex-wife has said about me."

He met her gaze, and she tried not to react. They were in their thirties. Divorce wasn't unheard of by any means. But she had to wonder about kids. He never mentioned any, but if he did have some, that would definitely change things. "You're divorced?"

"Yep."

"How long?"

"It was finalized last fall."

She lifted her eyebrows. "That's not been too long ago. Hang on, were you married when we…"

"No. It'd been over for quite a while before that. It was finalized in September of last year."

She nodded, relieved but still skeptical. And then a new thought hit her. "Was I your first, post-divorce?"

He looked at her intently. "If I say yes, is that a knock against me?"

"Well, it doesn't help your case. Of course you lingered on the thought of me. I was probably your first good sex in a long time…unless you were one of those couples who didn't get along but the sex was amazing."

"Not one of those couples."

She shrugged, secretly relieved. "It sounds like you quit giving her the attention she needed."

"That was her issue with me. One of them. There were many."

"Like you said, we're all flawed. Did you two do therapy and all that fun stuff?"

"We tried. But once we started talking about divorce, we

were both more interested in that idea than staying together."

"What would you get hyper-focused on? Another woman?"

"Nothing that exciting. Mostly work. I think that's what makes me a good programmer. And I'm team lead, so there are a lot of responsibilities that fall on me. A lot of late nights. A lot of missed opportunities." He bit his lip and she could see he wanted to tell her something.

"Opportunities at home?"

He met her gaze and his cheeks flushed. "Opportunities to procreate, I guess."

"Ah, you guys were trying to have kids. Of course you were."

"What do you mean by that?"

"It's standard issue. Almost every married couple I've ever known has had kids. It's always a shock to find one who hasn't had them."

"What about all your friends down here?"

She waved him off. "They're all pretty newly together. They'll get there."

"That's not what you want?"

"At the risk of sounding completely selfish, no. I don't see why everyone has to have kids. The world is perfectly populated. There're more than enough people willing to have them. I just don't happen to be one of them."

He lifted an eyebrow at her. "Do you want marriage?"

"I'm not opposed to marriage, but it's also not high on my agenda. I'll admit, it's not easy watching every friend I've ever had get married and start down the child path. But it's not changing who I am and what I want."

"What do you want?"

"I can tell you what I don't want."

"Okay."

"I don't want to bring a kid into a family and have her... or him, feel like they're responsible for me." She pointed at her chest. "I've got my own life under control. I don't need another human living their life for me." Her words came out a whole lot more passionate than she intended them to.

"Is that why you think some people have kids?"

"I know that's why some people have kids. People say it all the time. 'Who's gonna take care of me when I'm older? I've got to have kids so they'll do it.' Then they have five or six kids, and each of them thinks the other one is going to do the caretaking, so the parent ends up even more depressed because they couldn't get their six kids to love them." She thought about his aunt and cousins. "I didn't mean Kim. I hope you know that."

The server arrived with their drinks and set them down, saving Felicity from the awkward moment. Why had she never learned to shut up?

They both took a sip and then Scott nudged her with his knee, the velvet of his Santa suit rubbing up against her bare leg. "I didn't think you meant Kim, for the record. And even if you did, it's how you feel. There's no need to apologize for that."

Felicity liked this response. "That's another flaw of mine. I sometimes spew nonsense without realizing what I'm saying." She gauged him. "Is that what you and your ex were trying for? A big family?"

He gnawed on his lip. "We were trying to have kids. However, I wasn't really doing it for myself or my wife."

"Who were you doing it for?"

"At first, when we got married, I thought the idea of kids would be something I would get used to after we had time to chew on it. We agreed early on that we would have them, but not until later, and she was okay with that. She was career-focused as well. But then as all the couples around us started having them, she wanted them sooner."

"Was that okay with you?"

He shrugged. "I kept resisting, but then my mom got sick. She had to pull back from her work, which was everything to her, and she became almost obsessive about me giving her a grandkid."

"What was her work?"

He hesitated briefly. "She helped women get out of domestic abuse situations."

A cold chill went up her spine. She wasn't ready to share about her mother's situation, but it was quite a coincidence that his mother helped survivors for a living. But now that she thought about it, Scott was involved with Shayla because he was helping her out of a bad situation, so it sort of all made sense. "That sounds like important work."

"Definitely. About a year before she died, when she was still having moments of clarity once in a while, she became really depressed about having to quit her job. She made me promise to take up her life's work at some point."

"Is that something you'd like to do someday?"

He scratched his forehead. "I mean...sure. It sounds like good work. But..." He looked to be struggling for the words.

"You've got a job," she said, hoping to ease his guilt.

"Right," he said, but he still looked shamefaced. He closed his eyes tightly, shaking his head. "Anyway, my dad was gone and she had nothing, I guess I thought if I could just do this one thing for her—give her a grandchild—it would take some of the hurt of it all away." His Adam's apple bobbed, and she knew they were getting into some deep territory.

"That's a heavy burden to carry."

He just nodded and then took a drink of his beer.

"How do you feel about kids now that the pressure is off?" she asked.

"I don't know. I think I associate them with all that pressure and sadness. I think I'm more relieved that I don't have to deal with it or think about them."

"That makes perfect sense. And you're a guy. You can father children until you're seventy."

"It sort of drives me crazy when I hear young guys saying that they have to have kids in their twenties because they want to throw baseball with them or be active with them. So I'm gonna turn forty and suddenly be useless? I work out. I plan to stay in shape."

Lucky for her. She perused his biceps, though they were tucked away behind Santa suit velvet. "You look good."

He gave her a proud smile. "Thanks."

She looked down at her beer and then back at him. "That thing where you get hyper-focused on something... that's not what you're doing right now, is it?"

He gave her a confused look.

"Never mind." She wiggled in her seat, picking up her beer.

"Are you asking if I'm fixated on you?"

She shrugged. "I don't know. If this is an issue you have, maybe you're just trying to achieve the win and then you'll be on to the next fixation."

He leaned in. "If it is, then it's lasted over a year. I've never had a fixation that's lasted that long."

She narrowed her gaze at him. "So you've just been sitting up there in Nashville pining away over me for the past year?"

He leaned back. "Well, I didn't say that."

"Tell me about this past year."

"What do you wanna know about it?"

She considered him. "Fresh off a divorce. Pent up. Did you go all bachelor crazy—do any wild trips, parties, three-somes?" She wiggled her fingers at him. "Spill."

He shrugged. "I worked a lot."

She cocked her head to the side. "That's no fun. And I don't believe you."

"Okay, I did date some—kind of a lot, actually."

"Who did you date?"

He looked up at the ceiling. "A variety of women, really."

"Give me your top three."

He let out a sigh. "I don't know. I don't really want to talk about this."

"Sure you do. Did you hook up with any of them?" His face went red, and she smiled. "Scott, I hope you know you weren't cheating on me."

"I know. It's just kind of weird to talk about, don't you think?"

"I'm comfortable with it."

"My guess is you're comfortable with most things."

She waggled her eyebrows. "We're going there?"

He blushed again, looking down at his beer.

"Scott Stover, did I make you blush?"

"No," he said, smiling down at his beer.

"You weren't too vanilla as far as I remember."

"Hell no, I'm not."

She grinned at him and then took a drink of her beer.

He held her gaze. "What about you? What did this last year look like?"

"I don't know. Probably best to let your imagination run wild. Reality is probably not nearly as exciting as what you can conjure up."

"If you think I want to think about you with other guys, you're nuts."

"You wanna believe that I stayed home for over a year and didn't date anybody, had no hook ups?"

"That's exactly what I want to believe."

"Oh please. Then I would seem too available and you'd stop chasing."

"Has there been anyone significant?"

She shrugged, wanting to keep him guessing.

"More than one guy?"

"Which would be worse? One significant guy or a few randoms?"

"True, I don't like any of those prospects. Why don't you tell me when the last time was you had a hookup."

"We're going there, huh?"

"I just want to know if it was last week or last month."

She thought about how she wanted to answer. "I've been pretty chill since I got to town."

He paused, looking relieved. "When did you arrive?"

"October."

"So at least a couple of months. Are you sure you don't want to invite me back to your place?"

She tried hard to hold back her grin. "Keep it in your pants over there. You've got more chasing to do."

He smiled so wide dimples popped out she didn't know existed. "I do love the chase."

"Most men do."

"When's the last time a guy caught you, tied you down?"

She wiggled her shoulders. "Now we're getting to the fun talk."

"In a relationship."

"Oh," she said, letting her shoulders sag. "That's no fun."

"You do relationships, don't you?"

She shrugged.

He narrowed his gaze, turning his head to the side. "Seriously? You don't do relationships?"

"I have done them. They're just no fun."

"Maybe you haven't found the right guy to be in one with."

"That's for damn sure or I wouldn't be sitting here single."

"I have a feeling there have been many guys who've tried to tie you down and failed."

"A few have succeeded. I've got the video to prove it."

He shook his head, furrowing his brow. "I don't know that I've learned when to take you seriously or not."

"Good. Because it'll be boring once you figure me out."

He widened his smile. "I can't imagine any day with you would be boring."

She leaned in. "Then let's make sure we keep it interesting."

He met her in the middle. "Invite me home with you tonight and I'll show you just how interesting I can make you feel."

Heat rocketed through her core, waking up her senses in a way they hadn't been awakened since the last time she was with him. She slid off the bench. "You're getting warmer." She gave him a wink, and then walked off toward the ladies' room, sensing his stare on her backside and soaring higher than she had in a long time.

_____

10

When Felicity came out of the bathroom, a guy sitting at another bar table grabbed her attention. Scott moved to the edge of his seat, ready to rescue her, but then she seemed to gain recognition of who the guy was and wrapped her arms around him. Scott's neck went hot.

The guy looked her up and down, and she held up both hands, doing a twirl for him ending in a curtsy, holding her elf skirt out to the sides. Then two of them had a good laugh over it. Scott didn't think there was anything funny about Felicity putting her body on display for another man.

The guy looked to be introducing her to his friend, and she held out her hand, allowing him to shake it. Of course, the guy held her hand way too long. After a few more torturous minutes of this nonsense, she held up her hand in a wave and then walked away from the two of them and back to Scott.

She sat down at the table and eyed him curiously. "Are you okay? Did that beer hit you wrong?"

He got a hold of himself and straightened up. "No. I'm

good." But because he couldn't help himself, he asked, "Who is that guy?"

"Tom?"

Scott raised his eyebrows.

"He's one of Chase's investment partners."

Chase O'Neil would forever be a thorn in Scott's side. "You and Chase are pretty close, huh?"

"He's a friend."

"But to be fair, you've slept with him." He could tell by the look on her face that he screwed up. "I didn't mean that how it sounded. I just meant you were more than friends at some point."

"At some point over a year ago. More like a year and a half ago to be exact."

"How did all of that happen, anyway?"

She frowned at him. "How did all of what happen?"

He took a breath. "How did you meet him?"

"Maya and I were down here on vacation. We met him and Bo in a bar."

"You just walked up to him?"

"Well, to be technically correct, they walked up to us."

"Of course they did."

She leaned back, slack-jawed. "Please don't tell me you're jealous of a married man who is completely bonkers over his wife."

"I am not jealous of Chase O'Neil."

"Then why are you so interested in my relationship with him?"

He scratched his upper lip. "I saw Shayla the other day."

"You did?" she asked, looking rattled herself. Good. "Do you two hang out?"

"I went to see her at Harrison Pool Supply."

"How is she?"

"She's good. Pregnancy looks good on her."

"Of course it does. Does pregnancy ever not look wonderful on a woman?"

"Good point."

She made a motion with her hand. "So, you saw Shayla."

"Yeah."

"And?"

"And what?"

She looked exhausted with him. "She said something that bothered you. Something about Chase and me."

"She said the two of you were friends."

"Accurate."

"Do you want me to be honest with you?" he asked.

"No, I want you to lie to my face. Of course I want you to be honest."

"I find it hard to believe people who have slept together can be just friends."

She narrowed her gaze. "Are you telling me you have never remained friends with a woman who you slept with?"

He thought about it. "Actually, no."

"Seriously?"

"Seriously. When it's over, it's over."

"So you've only ever slept with people you've been in relationships with?"

"Yeah, or people I've dated," he said.

"You've never had a friend with benefits?"

He squinted. "How does that even work?"

She looked pleased with herself. "You've seriously never slept with a friend?"

"No."

"Why not?"

He squeezed his own leg out of frustration. "Maybe I'm not as enlightened as you are. I think sex opens up all kinds of complications. I can't have sex with somebody and then it not be awkward around them if we're not still having it."

She laughed at him which got his blood boiling.

"What is so damn funny?" he asked.

"You're very passionate, aren't you?"

He felt stung. "What's that supposed to mean?"

She studied him. "You're starting to make more sense to me now."

He was getting frustrated with her. "I don't know what you're doing, but you can stop it."

She wiggled in her chair. "Now this is getting interesting. You don't like that I can see you."

"Well of course you can. You're not blind as long as you've got your contacts in, right?"

"I think I'm starting to put some pieces together."

He harrumphed.

"You're passionate. That's part of why our weekend was so fabulous. Your passion was pretty unmatched. I thought this whole time that you were so full of lust because you were in love with Shayla, and with every move inside of me, you were pounding away at some love demon that was haunting you. But now I think I get it. Sex means something to you."

"Of course it fucking means something to me," he said, feeling the heat in his chest. Because it damn sure needed to mean something to her.

"But not always," she said.

"What are you talking about?"

"Apparently all year long you've been up there in Nashville thinking about me, yet there were a few girls you had no problem pounding."

He looked around, feeling out of control of this conversation.

"These were girls you liked. Women you thought were potential *someones*."

"Or maybe I was just picturing you."

She gave him a knowing look. "Oh, come on now, Scott," she said in a voice lower and more sensual than her regular magical voice somehow. "Do you think I'm going to be bothered by a couple of quick lays? Maybe I'm even a bit turned on by the idea of you driving into some woman while you think of me." She waggled her eyebrows.

He swallowed hard, wondering how he lived his entire life without knowing the vast extent of sexual prowess certain women actually held. "That turns you on?"

She bit her bottom lip, raising his cock, even in a Santa suit. "If I say yes, will you still respect me in the morning?"

"Invite me home tonight and let's find out."

"Well fuck me running. Look who it is." Scott felt a clasp on his shoulder and turned to find the most punchable face on the planet. His worst frenemy, Chase O'Neil.

"What are you doing here?" Felicity asked, hopping off her stool and hugging the six-and-a-half-foot tall goon. Theirs wasn't a quick hug. It was one with extra squeezes and rubs to the back. Images of the two of them in bed assaulted his brain like a tsunami of torture. They finally pulled apart and he held his giant hand out to Scott. As Scott imagined the places that man's hand had been on his woman, he grabbed it and squeezed, probably a little too hard. If Chase noticed, he didn't flinch.

"I was next door at a client's Christmas party, and my buddy texted me to come have a drink with him." Chase saw the same guy Felicity had talked to a minute ago and waved at him.

"Shouldn't you be at the Christmas party your company is hosting?" Scott asked.

"I was there. I had to leave right before you guys came on. I'm sorry I missed the show. How did it go?"

Felicity smiled at Scott. "He killed it as Santa."

"I'll bet he did," Chase said. "Seriously, man, thanks so much for stepping up. I was going to do it but I couldn't miss that other party. It was an important client and I needed to make an appearance."

"No problem. I was happy to do it."

Chase turned back to Felicity and looked her up and down. "I'll never be able to watch the movie *Elf* again without picturing this. Thanks a lot." He gave her a crooked smile, and she grinned back at him.

Scott ground his teeth.

"You two enjoy your evening," Chase said. "Good to see you both." He walked over to his friend, leaving them alone again.

Scott pointed at him. "Should he really be flirting with you? He's a married man."

She let her shoulders sag. "You cannot be serious. That was totally harmless."

"It was disrespectful to his wife."

"Do you seriously think Shayla is threatened by my relationship with Chase? She's the one who encourages us to get together."

Scott pursed his lips in concession. "I heard."

"She told you that?"

He adjusted himself in his seat. "Yeah, she said something like that. I think she sees your relationship with him kind of like she does mine with her."

"Except for the part where you fell in love with her. Chase and I were never in love."

"I told you I wasn't in love with her."

"Yeah, about that..."

He looked down at his beer, remembering what he had said to her back in the changing room about his complicated feelings for Shayla.

"Why did you think that what happened with Shayla and her ex was your fault?" she asked.

He let out a sigh. "Remember I told you I worked a lot of late nights?"

"Yeah. Were those with Shayla?"

"Not just with Shayla. Well, sometimes it was just her and me. But we were on the same team and worked on the same projects together. I guess you could say it triggered Brian."

"Scott, you can't believe that you had some fault in that abusive asshole's rage."

"I know. But I can't help but believe that if we hadn't been there working late that last time..." He stopped himself, realizing he was revealing too much information.

Felicity had her eyebrows knitted together, regarding him with concern.

"Never mind."

She looked down at her beer, twirling it at the base. He was glad to see that she knew when not to push.

"You haven't really had much of your beer," he said.

She smiled at him. "I don't really like it very much."

He grinned back at her. "The world makes more sense now."

"I tried to be unpredictable—wanted to throw you off your game."

"Oh believe me, woman, I have no clue what I'm doing with you."

She smiled even bigger. "You had a little bit of a clue a year ago."

"Just a little bit?"

"Maybe more than a little."

He sat back in his seat. "Anytime you're ready for round two, I'm good to go."

"I'll take that under advisement."

"You're going to make me work hard for it, aren't you?"

She leaned in. "You have no idea how hard I can make it." She gave him an alligator smile, and he knew if she didn't let him into her bed soon, he was wasn't getting out of this with his sanity intact.

11

"That was it? No sex?" Sebastian asked as he pulled into the Sweet Breezes Retirement Community.

"Not yet. I'm making him wait for it. You said he was patient."

"He may be, but I'm starting to get restless myself. I'm living my sex life vicariously through you these days."

"You've picked the wrong girl for that."

"How long has it been?"

She slid him a look. "You don't want to know."

"That long?"

"I gave up at some point this past year."

He wheeled into a parking place. "Did that have anything to do with the beautiful man you've been torturing this past week?"

"I don't think so," she said, wondering if that was a lie. "Maybe." He put the car in park and she grabbed his arm. "He was really good in bed, Sebastian. I mean *really* good. Honestly, the memory of it was enough to keep me going for the next few months, and then I moved back in with my mom for a while after my dad left, and things sort of shifted into a super nonsexual mode. I never really rebounded back into myself."

"Scott was your last?"

She pointed at him. "Don't you dare tell him or anyone else that."

He tossed both hands up like he was being arrested. "I would never."

They grabbed the pastries from the back seat and headed inside, stopping in front of an elderly black lady on the front porch. "Morning, Miss Mable." Sebastian air kissed her cheeks and handed her a pastry out of the bag along with a napkin.

"Morning, Sebastian. Who's this lovely lady with you, sweetheart?"

"This is Felicity. Felicity, meet Miss Mable."

"Ooh, aren't you a pretty little thing," Miss Mable said. "I've been telling Sebastian he needs to meet a nice girl and get married."

Sebastian widened his eyes and nodded at Felicity.

"Oh, yes, he's a great guy," she said, taking him by the arm and resting her head on his shoulder.

"We're going to see Ms. Martha and the crew. You enjoy the pretty day," Sebastian said.

"I will. I always love the warm weather."

Sebastian ushered Felicity down the hallway and to a room containing three elderly ladies sitting in wheelchairs watching television. "Hello, ladies, I want you to meet a good friend of mine. This is Felicity."

"Hello." Felicity made eye contact with each of them.

"Felicity, this is Martha, Geneva, and Thelma."

"My, my, Sebastian. She is as lovely as you described." Geneva spoke with a drawl that only came from the Deep South.

Martha rolled over to Felicity and touched her arm. "So have you had relations with that gorgeous man yet?"

Felicity gave Sebastian a look. "Seriously?"

"What can I say? I like to keep them updated."

Sebastian passed out pastries and napkins for everyone.

Thelma bit into a pastry. "That Seaside Sweets makes the most incredible cinnamon rolls I've ever laid in my mouth."

Martha shook her head, eyes closed in what looked like ecstasy. "I love these apple walnut scones."

Geneva waved a hand at Sebastian. "So how do you know this one?"

Sebastian put his hands on Felicity's shoulders. "This is my lifelong friend. We've known each other since our school days."

"I love that," Martha said. "I hope you'll always stay friends."

"We will," they both said in unison, smiling at one another. The love Felicity felt for Sebastian was deeper than any love she'd ever experienced, outside of her mother.

Sebastian handed Felicity a brush and nodded toward Martha. He sat down on the edge of the bed and started brushing Thelma's hair out with soft slow strokes.

Felicity followed suit and sat behind Martha. She held a lock of hair loosely and began slowly stroking it with the brush. "Is this okay, Miss Martha?"

"Yes, sweetheart, that feels nice."

An orderly came in with some rolls of toilet paper, and Thelma said, "Honey, is Doctor Baldwin still here?"

"I think so," the orderly said, heading into the bathroom.

"Will you please send him back down here a minute? I have one more question about my hip."

"Yes, ma'am," the girl said and headed out.

Sebastian spilled the tea about the ladies. Felicity learned about their husbands, when they died, and how many kids each of the ladies had. He knew the names and ages of each lady's grandchildren, and a few great-grandchildren. It was clear he had spent countless hours in that room with them and had taken care to make sure each of these women were made to feel special when he was there.

He motioned her to start on Geneva's hair. He moved over to Martha and began creating braids and pinning them up in a bun. In a bit, a tall, fit, blond-headed man with a lab coat on came into the room, typing into a tablet without looking up. "You had a question, Ms.—" As he glanced up, making out Felicity and Sebastian, he seemed to be taken off guard. "Oh, hello. I'm Doctor Baldwin." He held out his hand to Sebastian, who had his hands full of hair that clearly could not be dropped.

"Hmm, how about an elbow bump," Sebastian said, offering the handsome doctor his elbow.

The doctor blinked and then awkwardly tapped his elbow to Sebastian's.

"I'm Sebastian."

The doctor's eyes widened, and then he crossed his arms over his chest with a curious smile. "Oh, okay. You're not what I was picturing."

"You were picturing me? I hope I'd shaved." Sebastian gave the doc an easy smile and then focused on Thelma's hair.

The doctor stared at Sebastian, open-mouthed, like he was looking at a celebrity. Sebastian was either utterly clueless to this guy's obvious attraction to him, or he was playing cool.

"Sebastian comes to see us a few times a week," Geneva said.

"Yes, I've heard. You're the one plying my patients full of pastries."

Sebastian glanced around the room. "Who wants me to stop?" When nobody raised their hand, Sebastian cut his gaze back to the doctor. "You're outnumbered."

"I can see that," the doctor said, smiling at Sebastian like a flirty teenage girl.

When the silent sexual tension was more than even Felicity could bear, she spoke up. "I'm Felicity."

The doctor pried his gaze away from Sebastian and blinked Felicity into focus. "Sure, sorry. I'm Doc...Flynn."

"Doctor Flynn?" Felicity asked, wondering if she'd misheard him before.

"No, just Flynn. That's my first name."

"As in Errol," Geneva said with a twinkle in her eye.

He glanced over at Sebastian who was focused on Thelma and whispering something in her hear that made her giggle.

Flynn furrowed his brow at Felicity. "Are you and Sebastian..."

"No, God no. Just friends."

Sebastian glanced up at the doctor quickly, and then back to Thelma's hair. Hopefully it was just in time to catch the look of relief on the doc's face.

Flynn shook his head like he was reorienting himself and then checked his tablet. "What was the question you had, Ms. Peterson?"

"Oh, you know what, I can't even remember. Must be my senility." Thelma winked at Sebastian who gave her a warning glance.

"Right," Flynn said, holding the tablet with both hands over his stomach. "If you remember, I'll be here a few more minutes. I was going to grab some lunch in the cafeteria before I head out. I think it's salmon croquette day."

"Yes," Martha said. "Sebastian, you like salmon croquettes, don't you?"

Sebastian shot her a look, speechless for maybe the first time in his life.

"Well, it was nice meeting you both. Take care," the doc said, his gaze lingering on Sebastian as he exited the room.

"Mmm-hmm," Sebastian said, barely giving him a parting glance.

They all stayed perfectly still and quiet until the footsteps faded down the hallway.

"So as I was saying— ow!" Sebastian cried, clearly feeling the sting of Thelma's pinch.

Thelma glared in his direction. "Why didn't you give that poor boy your attention?"

"I've told you all. No doctors. They have God complexes and are way too ego-driven."

"Not this one," Martha said. "Doctor Baldwin is sweet and kind. He listens to everything we have to say."

"And we say a lot more than what a doctor should be forced to listen to," Geneva said.

"Amen to that," Martha said. "Go eat some salmon with that poor young man."

"He didn't look too poor to me," Sebastian said. "I saw his shoes."

Felicity could tell this was going to take some massaging. She squeezed Martha's shoulders. "Will you all excuse me? I need to find a ladies' room."

"There's one right there," Sebastian said pointing at the bathroom in their suite.

"I need one down the hall. I think my granola cereal is

catching up with me. And thanks for making me have to explain that, by the way," she said, giving him a glare.

He pursed his lips at her, and she headed out of the room, hustling down the hallway, asking a nurse where she could find the cafeteria.

Sure enough, the good doctor was settling in at a table, pulling out his tablet. Felicity made a beeline for him. Sebastian was no fool. She probably only had so much time.

"Hello, Flynn, isn't it? Or is it Finn?"

"Flynn with an L," the guy said, glancing behind her.

She scooted into a chair. "We're short on time, so I hope you don't mind my bluntness. You're single, right?" She indicated his empty ring finger.

"Yes, but—"

"And just so we're clear, you're gay?"

He cleared his throat, glancing around. "Yes, but I don't typically introduce myself that way."

"Of course you don't." She pulled a pen out of her purse and then snatched one of his napkins. "This is the number of that very handsome man back there. He's the most incredible man you've ever met." She stopped and looked him in the eye. "And that is not some bullshit I'm feeding you with rose-colored glasses on. You will never in your life meet a man more brilliant, funny, and compassionate as him. So, I highly suggest you give him a call."

He leaned in. "He didn't seem very receptive to me."

"He's a tough nut to crack, but worth every bit."

"How do you know I'd be any good for him?"

"I don't, but those women seem to think you hung the moon. And they love Sebastian like a son. I doubt they would hang him out to dry." She finished writing down the number and then shoved it his way. "I'm taking a chance."

She glanced around to find Sebastian standing in the

doorway of the cafeteria. "Did you get lost looking for the ladies'?" Sebastian asked, fist on his hip, eyebrows up.

"Time's up," Felicity said, giving Flynn a wink. "Don't screw this up." She turned around and walked toward Sebastian, adjusting her purse strap as she brushed past him. "I was in the mood to grab a croquette myself."

"Did you just give that man my phone number?" he asked, marching beside her.

"You know I would never do something like that."

"I know you would do exactly that. I told you, no doctors."

"Even cute available ones? He's gorgeous. What is wrong with you?"

"They're full of themselves. I can't handle such a fragile ego."

She stopped and turned toward him, directing him over to the side of the hallway. "I think what you can't take is the idea of allowing yourself to be loved."

He cocked his head to the side, giving her a lazy stare. "What is this, Therapy 101? My daddy didn't love me so I can't let anyone in? I think we're past that."

She took him by the shoulders. "Sebastian, you hate dating apps with a passion. You only go to gay bars when it's all of us together and you never hit on anybody or allow yourself to be hit on. When are you ever going to have a chance like this again?"

He let out an exhaustive sigh. "I don't even know if he's gay."

"He's gay. I just confirmed."

He shook his head at her and then slid his arm into hers, directing them back to the room. "Why do I put up with you?"

She grinned, more excited about the idea of Sebastian potentially finding love than she could contain.

"You better hope I don't interfere with your love life the way you have with mine today. I have dirt on you now, you know?"

She jerked her head toward him. "You wouldn't?"

Just as they were getting ready to step back into the room, he said, "Oh I wouldn't? Keep your guard up, Miss Priss."

A woman looking like she was a few years shy of being a patient there herself stood in the middle of the room holding a clipboard. "Sebastian, I was just looking for you."

"Yes, Miss Barb, what can I do for you?"

"We're organizing carolers for some shut-ins in each of the neighborhoods around 30A, and we're looking for volunteers to chair each section. Can I count on you for Seacrest?"

"Absolutely."

"Perfect." She handed him a piece of paper and then turned to Felicity. "What neighborhood do you live in, hon?"

"Oh, I don't—"

"Santa Rosa. She can cover Blue Mountain," Sebastian said. "And she's more than happy to help."

The woman flipped through her papers and then handed one to Felicity. "Wonderful. Thank you both. My number is on the sheet if you have any questions."

She scooted out the door and Felicity looked at Sebastian with wide eyes.

"It's Christmas," he said. "It's the time for giving, including our time."

The sheet had a list of addresses along with a date and time and list of suggested songs.

"This is legit? These people want us to roll up on them singing Christmas carols?"

"Absolutely," Geneva said. "These people are lonely. They think they want to live at home, but they don't know how nice it can be when you make friends at a place like this." She looked at the other two women and they smiled at each other. Felicity's heart grew two sizes, not unlike the Grinch's.

"Fine," she said to Sebastian. "But we're even now."

"Merry Christmas, my love," he said, bringing her in for a hug. She held onto him tightly, her mind a whirlwind of family, love, loss, and all the things she did and did not have this Christmas. She decided to sweep away all the bad and be thankful for the love of a good friend. "Merry Christmas."

12

Scott had no idea what he was walking into. When Felicity had sent him a text asking him how his baritone was, and he replied with *subpar*, he got another text with a date, time, and location. When he asked more questions, he didn't get any answers. He didn't know if she was simply a bad texter, or if she was as full of mystery as he suspected she was.

She'd dropped him off after their time at the bar the night of the Christmas party, and despite her telling him numerous times that she wasn't going to invite him home with her, he'd still held out hope. Their conversation had veered toward the naughty more than a few times, to his delight. But she still wasn't ready to open herself up to him. There had to be a reason why. And he had to get to the bottom of it, which was why he found himself blindly showing up at the address she had specified in her text.

He walked up to the parking lot to find a van with Chase O'Neil's face plastered on the side. He should've figured he couldn't take a dump in this town without having to deal with that guy.

Felicity stood chatting with a group of people, most of whom looked a few years younger than the two of them. She met his gaze and gave him that sneaky smile that said she was up to something.

"I wasn't sure if you would show," she said as he walked up to her.

"I wasn't sure if I had a choice."

"You always have a choice, man," a guy with shaggy brown hair said to him, and then held out a hand. "Logan."

"Scott," he said.

A guy who towered over all of them just like Chase O'Neil did, stepped in. "Chapman. You don't wanna hear me sing."

A leggy blonde slid her arm around Chapman's waist. "He's not that bad. Me on the other hand? Horrendous. You've all been warned," she said pointing a finger around their group.

"That's Taylor," Felicity said, and the pretty blonde nodded at him.

Next to her was Raven, the woman who was planning his aunt's party. "Hi, Scott, do you remember me? I'm working with your aunt on your party," Raven said, holding out a hand.

He shook it. "Of course. This is your crew?"

"I would've asked my own friends," Felicity said, "but each one of them is organizing their own caroling in a different community around 30A this evening."

"How many other communities are doing this?" the tall blonde asked.

Felicity looked up at the sky and counted off on her fingers. "Seanna and Blake are doing Seaside, Sebastian's doing Seacrest, Shayla and Chase are doing Seagrove, Marigold and Dane are doing WaterColor, Cassidy and

Jesse are doing Grayton Beach, and Meade and Ryder are doing Rosemary Beach."

"What about Bo and Maya?" Scott asked, knowing they lived in Panama City.

"Present and accounted for," came Bo's voice from behind him. Scott turned around, relieved to see a familiar face. He went to shake Bo's hand, and Bo brought him in for a hug. Scott guessed they were on hugging terms now.

Maya and Felicity hugged as well. "How are you?" Maya asked, holding onto Felicity tightly.

"I'm good." She pulled away and squeezed Maya's shoulders, a significant look passing between them. Scott figured they were close friends since they had been on vacation down there together, but he had not gotten their full story yet.

Felicity addressed the group as a whole. "We ready to go sing?"

"Yep," a few of them said, and then Felicity slid open the door to the van. "Hop in."

They all piled in, and Scott got in the front seat next to Felicity. She cranked up the engine and then handed him a folded-up sheet of paper. "The addresses are on there. Will you be my navigator?"

"Sure thing," he said, pulling up the GPS on his phone. It directed Felicity where to turn. "You were kind of secretive about what we were doing tonight."

"I was afraid to use the word *caroling*. I didn't know if you'd come."

"You invited me. You knew I would come."

She cut him a glance with a little grin.

They pulled up to the first house and piled out. "Do you have that piece of paper I handed you in the car with the addresses?" Felicity asked.

"Yep," Scott said, unfolding it.

Felicity stood beside him, looking down at the piece of paper. There was that cherry almond smell again. That scent buried itself deep inside of him. He would never smell it again without thinking of her.

"Okay, folks," Felicity said. "This is Mr. Cook. He loves 'Up on the Housetop.' Raven started a group chat for us, and she's texting the lyrics now."

Scott's phone dinged, and there was a link to the song.

Felicity counted them off, and they all started singing, sounding like a bunch of cows mooing. In a bit, the front door opened and a man eased out, using a cane. He stood, watching the group with a smile on his face as they went through the entire song. When they finished, Felicity, Raven, and Maya walked up to him, Raven holding a paper plate of cookies.

Bo Harrison sidled up to Scott. "Is this your first time to carol?"

"I've got to say it is. What about you?"

"No, I get roped into this every year. I don't do much though throughout the year other than throw money at charities. I guess it feels good to actually get my ass out of the house and be a part of something with the community."

"Yeah, I guess it does feel pretty good."

"I heard you played Santa at Chase's party the other night."

Scott didn't like the fact that the party was being contributed to Chase when all he did was pay for it. "It was nice getting to talk to some of the families. The kids were cute."

"I'll bet."

They stood and watched the women chatting up the old man. Scott decided to take this opportunity with Bo to grab some intel. "You met your wife when she was down here on vacation with Felicity, right?"

"Yeah, about a year and a half ago. They were here visiting Sebastian. But it was kind of funny. Chase and I met the two of them in a bar and had no idea who they were here visiting. Then we met up again at Sebastian's house. He had planned on fixing her up with me for the week. Didn't even know I already met her."

"That worked out pretty nicely."

"It was a fun week, I'll tell you that." He smiled, looking to be remembering something fondly.

"I guess the four of you hung out all week that week then, huh?" Scott asked, torturing himself with the idea Felicity and Chase together.

"Yeah. I thought I was done dating tourists until Maya came along." Bo smiled like a sucker in love.

"Those two are good friends?"

"Yeah, Felicity and Maya grew up together in Indianapolis, Sebastian too. The three of them have been tight since they were kids."

"It's always good to have a lifelong friend."

"New friends can be pretty cool too," Bo said, giving him a quick look. Bo had been described by Blake once as having a heart of gold. Scott could see bits and pieces of that in Bo in subtle ways.

"How did this whole group of yours get together?" Scott asked.

"Really, I guess it was all Chase. I knew him from both of us owning small businesses in town and being a part of that community, and then Chase met Blake doing handyman work on his properties."

"Blake the doctor?"

Bo waved him off. "It's a long story. Boring."

Scott had a feeling the story wasn't boring at all.

"Anyway, Blake knew Cassidy because he did handyman work for her at her bakery, and Cassidy knew Sebastian because he's a regular there at Seaside Sweets, and then we all kind of intertwined from there, bringing people in different ways."

"That's nice. It's not always easy to make friends outside of work as an adult."

"That's true. I like the guys who work for me, but I'm the boss. I know they feel like they have to hold back certain things. I like this crew. We're all real different, but the friendships seem to work somehow." Bo cut his gaze at Scott. "I see you're hanging with Felicity again." He raised an eyebrow.

Scott shrugged. "Trying to. She's a bit of a closed book. Do you know her very well?"

"I got to know her a bit when I was living in Indianapolis for a few months." He smiled, shaking his head. "She's a whole lot of fun."

Scott's chest burned as he wondered if Bo had been with her too. But surely not.

"She's been real helpful to Maya since she's been here. We've been going through some stuff."

Scott shuffled, not sure how to respond to that.

"Baby-making problems," Bo said. "Don't ask."

Scott blinked. "I've been there."

"Oh yeah?" Bo asked, looking confused.

"I'm divorced. We were trying. It pretty much killed our marriage."

Bo frowned.

"Not that I'm saying it will do that to yours. You guys are solid. She and I weren't solid before we started trying. And we were trying for the wrong reasons."

Bo nodded. "It's not easy, is it?"

"Not at all. The pressure. Fuck."

Bo's eyes got wide. "Fuck is right."

"Not to mention that you feel like less of a man."

Bo narrowed his gaze.

Scott tossed up a hand. "I did. Not saying you do."

Bo leaned in. "Of course I fucking do," he said in a whisper.

Scott glanced up and down his solid frame. The guy looked like he lived in a gym. "There's nothing wrong with your manhood, dude. Not that I'm getting weird on you or anything."

Bo looked down his nose at him. "Thanks, man. I needed that."

"No problem," Scott said, pocketing his hands, feeling a little awkward and a little helpful all at once.

"Did you guys deal with miscarriage, if you don't mind me asking?" Bo asked.

"We never got that far. Never got pregnant." Scott left out the fact that he was intensely relieved by that fact.

Bo huffed. "I don't know which is worse."

"It all sucks," Scott said. Bo's neck went red. "I'm sorry."

"Thanks," Bo said, biting his lip.

Scott had the urge to give him a hug, but they'd just become hello and goodbye huggers. They weren't *I'm sorry you've dealt with miscarriage* huggers just yet.

They stood in silence staring at the women for a moment, and then Bo said, "Ask Felicity about true crime podcasts."

"Really?"

"Yeah, she and I used to text about them all the time. She loves reading those crime books that are for women."

Scott frowned, trying to understand what he meant.

"Domestic thrillers is what she calls them. I think she's

read every one that's ever been put out. She's always trying to get me to read them, but I'm good with the podcasts."

"Noted."

"And she loves shows that have some kind of supernatural creature in them but aren't too serious. Anything that's got a lot of wit. You've got to be funny around her or she's not interested."

"Fuck," Scott said under his breath. "I'm not that funny." He thought about Chase and how he had the rep as being the funny guy in the group.

"You're plenty funny," Bo said.

Scott shrugged.

"And she loves farts."

Scott cocked his head to the side. "Now I know you're fucking with me."

"No, man, I'm totally serious. She thinks they're hilarious. I've gotten where I'll do it now just to make her laugh."

"And Maya is okay with that?"

"Do you think Maya's not used to my sense of humor by now?"

Scott lifted his eyebrows in concession. "But for the record, I'm not farting around her at this point."

"Tell her a fart joke. She'll love it."

Scott narrowed his gaze at Bo. "Just exactly how was it that you got Maya to go on a date with you?"

Bo grinned, and put his attention back on his wife.

THEY HIT SEVERAL MORE HOUSES, singing and passing out cookies, socializing with the shut-ins. Most were elderly, but a few were younger people with health issues. Scott was overcome with gratitude for his own health and vowed to do more to help others. He thought about his vow to his mother to take up her life's work of helping domestic violence survivors.

Helping Shayla out of her relationship and the emotions that came with it had drained him mentally to the point of exhaustion. He had such a huge respect for his mother and all she did to help people, but he never felt the calling like she had.

She'd grown up with an abusive father and seen things Scott couldn't fathom. She had something in common with the survivors, being one herself. Her mother's death at the hands of her own husband pushed his mom into the work and drove her to keep doing it no matter how hard it was.

Scott had grown up well-adjusted and happy for the most part. He wasn't sure he was the right person to take on that kind of work, but his guilt at his still-unfulfilled promise kept him feeling like he needed to make a plan to move toward that work one day, and sooner rather than later.

They piled out of the van in the parking lot where they first met up, and Felicity thanked everyone, giving each of them a hug.

Scott shook Bo's hand. "Good to see you, man."

"Good to see you too. Good luck with that thing we were talking about."

"Yeah, same to you." Bo winked at him and he and his wife were off.

Scott turned to Felicity, feeling like a sixteen-year-old kid weighing whether or not he had the balls to go in for a kiss. "This night turned out not to be what I thought it was going to be."

"What did you think it was going to be?"

"I had no idea. But I didn't expect to leave feeling moved."

Felicity let her shoulders sag and widened her eyes. "I know, right? I thought I was just organizing addresses on paper, but then talking to those people was really something special. I want to come back and visit them all again."

"I'll come with you if you do."

She gave him a sweet smile. He didn't see that one as often as he did her sneaky one. She looked down, scratching her forehead, which seemed to be her nervous move.

He needed to take the reins before she slipped away. "Want to get a Christmas drink? I'm sure we can find a bar with some eggnog somewhere."

"I need to return Chase's van."

"I'll help you. You'll need a ride once you drop it off, right?"

"Chase said he would take me home."

"Why bother him when I'm happy to help?"

She studied him and then slowly smiled, glancing away.

"What?" he said, unable to help a chuckle.

"You think this is your chance to find out where I live, don't you?"

He shrugged. "Just a good side effect."

She shook her head. "No way."

He laughed again. "Why don't you want me to see where you live?"

"Because I don't want you coming over for a late-night booty call whenever you please."

"Damn. You really think I would do that without checking in with you first?"

"I don't know. I don't really know you all that well."

"I've been trying to fix that."

Something about the way she smiled at him gave him a

green light, or at least a flashing yellow one. He moved a step closer to her. "I think you're afraid I'll come over and you'll let me in."

She slung the key ring around her finger, taking a step backward, bouncing off the van. She turned around and looked at it as if it had jumped out at her, and then rested against it, putting her fingertips to her forehead. She was nervous. He'd taken her off guard. This night got better and better as it went.

She pointed at him "I have plenty of willpower. Don't even try to test me."

He took her hand, rubbing his thumb over the top of it. "Are you sure about that?"

She swallowed hard, holding his gaze. A little grin slipped before she twirled herself out of his space. "Follow me to Chase's office, but only to return the car," she said, walking around to the driver's side.

He grinned like a moron all the way to his car.

13

F elicity cursed herself the whole way to Chase's office. She knew better than to invite Scott. But somehow, the thought of not inviting him was like dangling a cup of ice water in front of someone stuck in the desert for days.

How was she letting herself fall for him? Nobody was talking about love. That was insane. But she was letting herself want him...allowing her body to go tingly in places she was trying to shut off.

Maybe it was because she'd been with him before and she knew he was a passionate lover. He'd blown her away the first go-around. She had expected a quick and easy lay to help ease the disappointment of losing the idea of Chase, but what she'd gotten had woken her up from her core to the tips of her toes.

After being with Scott, she was fully aware that a relationship of friendly convenience wasn't going to fly with her. She'd hoped she would find that spark with someone else, maybe someone closer to home, at least someone she could easily enjoy a fuck-buddy-type relationship with...someone she could have whenever she wanted, at least until the sensation of the drug wore off.

He was reminding her what it felt like to feel alive. She'd not been fully awake this past year. She'd been existing. But here he was, ready to wake her ass up. She didn't know if she could handle riding that high and then absorbing the disappointment of falling back into those dull routines and mindset once the relationship crashed and burned as it inevitably would. But how could she keep turning him down when he was such a tempting carrot?

She parked the van and dropped the keys off in the slot where Chase had told her to drop them. When she headed toward Scott's car, she found him standing by the passenger side, opening the door. He wasn't for real with this chivalry. He was trying to get her in bed. She had no illusions. Still, she was falling for it hook, line, and sinker.

"I'm not a fan of eggnog," she said, as she slid into the passenger seat.

"I'm sure we can find something else to satisfy you," he said, shutting the door behind her.

Her heart pounded as she pulled the seatbelt over her chest. She had to get control of the situation. When he got in the car, she said, "There's this life-size gingerbread house I want us to go to."

He cocked his head at her like a confused puppy.

There was nothing like a bunch of kids running around with sticky hands to turn the mood off. That's what she needed if she was going to spend time with him.

"Okay," he said slowly.

"It's about twenty minutes away. Head toward Destin."

He followed her directions, and they found themselves in the parking lot of a high-end hotel on the beach.

He raised an eyebrow at her. "Are you sure we're going to find a life-sized gingerbread house in there?"

"That's what Maya said. She and Bo took their nephews here the other day. She was telling me about it this evening."

They headed to the lobby, and sure enough, there it was, front and center. The smell of gingerbread cookies filled the air. She turned to Scott. "You hungry?"

"I better be. That's a big cookie right there."

A handful of people milled around, observing and sniffing the sweet structure made of gingerbread bricks and icing for grout. Gumdrops and sprinkles covered the structure along with hard candies and marshmallows.

Scott held out an arm toward the entryway. "Shall we?"

"Let's do it," Felicity said, stepping into the sweet structure.

A colorful Christmas tree stood in the middle with a train choo-chooing around it. A mechanical toy elf climbed a ladder, perpetually staying in the same place, while a deep recorded voice bellowed, "Ho ho ho! Merry Christmas!" over the tune of "It's the Most Wonderful Time of the Year."

"Somebody put a lot of work into this," Felicity said.

"No doubt." Two little kids brushed past them as they ran circles around the tree, throwing Felicity off kilter in her heeled boots. Scott caught her as she put out her hand to steady herself on the Christmas tree, which would've been disastrous.

He looked down at her. "I guess we're in their territory."

"I did ask for it."

They stepped toward the back of the house, finding two exits. One was labeled *Family Fun Time This Way*, the other boasting *Lovers Lane This Way*.

Out the family exit, screeching kids ran circles around

their weary parents, while the Lovers Lane exit remained blissfully empty.

"Lady's choice," Scott said.

"Is there really a choice?"

Scott smiled and followed her out the Lovers Lane exit. They walked down a faux-candlelight lit red carpet path.

"Maya did not mention this."

"If they were with their nephews, they probably took the family exit to some activity somewhere."

"True. Where do you think this is taking us?"

They entered an open door to what must've been one of the hotel's conference rooms and found themselves in a tropical paradise. Lush plant life filled the room, covered in twinkly lights and bows. "Now this is more like it," Scott said.

They walked toward a small gazebo with a sign that said *Enter Here* above the arched entranceway.

They stepped inside, and when they did, lights gave the illusion of snow coming down from the ceiling. When Felicity looked up, she found mistletoe hanging above them. Her heart thumped.

She met his gaze. "It was a trap."

"Lucky for me."

She pursed her lips at him, knowing what was coming.

He held up a hand. "I don't make the rules."

"I know you're hating this."

"It's terrible, being forced to kiss the woman I haven't been able to get off my mind for the past year. What did I do to deserve this?" He slid his hands around her waist, and her whole body tensed with anticipation.

He leaned down, pressing his lips against hers, and she was transported back in time to their first kiss in Chase's guest room that Friday night of the wedding weekend. Even though they had said good night, she'd heard a knock on her door just as she was settling into bed, and she'd been happy to let him in. There'd been little preamble. They'd been flirting at the bar earlier and she'd made it clear she was interested in him.

But she'd made him wait this go-around, had him work for it. It was much safer the other way. No feelings involved. Just a primal urge to be satisfied at the hands of one another. But now, her feelings were involved. Danger lurked in that mistletoe above their heads, and she was powerless to stop it.

She pulled away, realizing she had grabbed a handful of his short hair at the base of his neck and dropped it like a hot potato, stepping back.

He looked at her in breathless curiosity. The kiss had gotten intense quickly, and she had not planned on that. She had no control over herself around him.

"Is it hot in here? I'm hot." She stepped out of the gazebo and made a beeline for the exit, which deposited her onto a sidewalk. She gripped the railing as the ocean lapped the shore in the near distance.

She heard the opening and shutting of the door and then felt his hand on her back. "You okay?"

She nodded. "I'm good." She smiled at him to punctuate her point, but by the look on his face, she was a terrible liar.

He pointed his thumb over his shoulder. "I'm sorry if I did something wrong back there."

"No. You didn't. You're pretty perfect, unfortunately."

He chuckled. "No one's ever called me that before."

She let out a sigh, shaking her head at herself. What was she getting into?

He nudged her hip. "It was just a kiss. It doesn't have to be anything more than that."

She looked up at him. "What if I want it to be?"

He lifted his eyebrows. "We are in a hotel."

She focused on her breathing, staring at him. Could it be that easy? Could they walk into that lobby and with one swipe of a credit card be together for the night? Could she allow such insanity?

No way. She was afraid if she got in bed with Scott, she would never be able to walk away again. And that posed all kinds of problems.

She pulled out her phone before she did something stupid. "You know what, this has been wonderful. And thank you so much for bringing me here, but I'm going to get a rideshare home."

"Wait, really?"

She couldn't look at him. She just thumbed in her order and was given the message that her ride was one minute away. This was a hotel, so there was probably a driver in the area already from a drop off.

She put her phone in her purse and then met his gaze. "Yes, but believe me when I say this, because no one's ever said it and meant it more than I do right now. It's not you. It's me." She hustled back inside to the lobby as quickly as she could, hoping he wouldn't follow.

The driver dropped her off at her long-term rental, and she glanced around as she hurried inside, wondering if Scott had followed them. Now she was being paranoid. She was literally afraid that love...or at least intense lust...was following her home.

She opened the door of the condo and dropped her keys and purse on the kitchen bar, pulling out her phone. She walked directly to the sliding glass door and made her way out to the balcony overlooking the shore, thanks to Chase. This was one of his rentals, and he was letting her have it for a steal. She would never have been able to afford this place on her own.

She collapsed in an Adirondack chair and bounced her phone on her thigh as she watched the surf roll in. Even though it was dark, a couple sat in beach chairs by the shore. How were they able to surrender to one another...to give themselves to each other along with all of their baggage for the other one to absorb?

She stared at her phone with a sense of dread mixed with worry overcoming her like her heart was being torn out of her chest. She pulled up her mom's name and called her.

"Hey honey," came her mom's sweet voice.

"Hi, Mama," she said. At some point, her friends in high school had changed their Mommies and Mamas to Moms, but there was no name for Felicity's mother other than Mama.

"How's my girl? Are you still loving it down there?"

"It's beautiful. I wish you would join me."

"You know I can't do that. I've got work."

"You can get a job at a grocery store down here, or move on to the next phase in your life."

"Honey, I've been at this same workplace since high school. Nobody's gonna pay me what I make now walking in somewhere else new."

"They might if you come in as a manager."

"I can't do that."

"Why not? Everyone knows you run that place now."

"Maybe in theory, but not in title. I'm still just a cashier."

Felicity closed her eyes tightly. Her mother's satisfaction with keeping the same job she'd had since high school was something Felicity couldn't reconcile, no matter how hard she tried.

"Besides," her mother said, "you know there are other reasons why I can't leave here."

Felicity shook her head. She would never understand why her mother felt such intense loyalty to her father. "How's...Pete?" Felicity asked through gritted teeth.

After her father had finally moved out of the house nine months ago, Felicity had thought her mother could heal. Then she met her mother's new boyfriend, and Felicity's world had been snatched from her. Felicity had believed her entire life that it was simply a matter of getting her mother away from her father. But once she had accomplished that, her mother moved onto a man exactly like him, or at least that's what the bruise on her mom's arm told her. Felicity now understood the problem was rooted so much deeper than removing one man.

"He's okay, I guess," her mom said.

Felicity perked up. "Is he still living with you?"

"I haven't seen him in a while, but he's got stuff here."

"Oh." Felicity didn't know how to interpret her mom's tone. She seemed more confused than anything. "Is that upsetting to you?"

"Well, I think it would've been respectful to let me know where he was going."

Ya think, Felicity wanted to say, but she kept her sarcasm to herself. "He just up and left?"

"I don't know, maybe. How's your job going?"

Deflection. It was what her mother did best. "It's good."

"You're still at the catering company?"

"A couple of them, really. I'm still doing shifts at the original place I told you I was working, but I'm also working with my friend Raven. She's starting her own catering company. I'm helping out with the overall party planning portion of it."

"That's ambitious. Do you think she can handle it?"

"I think she'd do better with a business partner. But yeah, she can handle it."

"How about you?" her mother asked.

Felicity's heel tapped on the floor. "I think she'd like me to be her partner." She wasn't sure why she had said it. Part of it was her way of lashing out and being passive aggressive. These were the kinds of games she played with her mother. The underlying text was *I have things I want to do in my life too, but you're holding me back.* Because even though she loved her mother with great intensity, their relationship did not come without its resentment on Felicity's part.

"That's wonderful news. I've always known you could be a business owner."

Felicity sighed, frustrated as usual. "You know I can't leave Indy long-term," she said, throwing her mom's words back at her.

"Well, of course you can. There's nothing holding you here."

Felicity wanted to scream, *You are holding me there!* After the realization that the cycle was going to continue, Felicity couldn't spend another ounce of energy trying to convince her mother to walk away from yet another man, continuing to enable the behavior. That's why she had made her escape, albeit temporary, to Santa Rosa.

But sooner or later, her father would be back in the picture. Or another man would be there treating her mom like shit, and she'd get a phone call from a hospital, telling her they required someone to drive her mom home before she could be released. That's why Felicity had been working a job that she could walk away from at any second. She had one foot out the door and the other foot pulling her back to this area where she wanted to be more than any place in the world.

"How about coming down for Christmas?" Felicity asked.

"Oh, I don't know. That sounds pretty extravagant."

"I'll get you a flight down. They're not too expensive. And you've already got a place to stay. Why wouldn't you come?"

"We'll see."

Felicity knew that meant we'll see what happens with whatever man is in her life at the moment, whether it be her dad or Pete or some other random guy who got his hooks into her.

"Ooh, I'm getting a call, hon. I'll talk to you soon, okay?" her mother said.

"Wait, Mama—"

But Felicity could tell she'd already disconnected. Dammit. It was probably her father or Pete or some other asshole her mother was taking up with. Who else would her mother diss her only child for in a heartbeat? Felicity let her head loll back, feeling out of control as she always did when it came to her mother.

14

Felicity lay on a chaise lounge with Sebastian by her side in front of his cabana on the beach, rubbing sunscreen on her legs. Though it was December, it was Florida, and the sun was out. She removed her crocheted cover-up to rub some on her arms.

"What's up there, Casper?" Sebastian asked. "You know you can let a little sun in."

"Not on these arms." She pulled her wide-brimmed hat down to ensure it covered her face. "We're thirty-six now. It's an uphill battle from here." She tossed the sunscreen into her bag. "So, what's happening with the good doctor?"

Sebastian pursed his lips, and she knew there was a story there.

She nudged him. "He called, didn't he?"

"Texted, sweetie. We're not in the nineties anymore."

"I mean called on you, like a proper suitor." She waggled her eyebrows.

"You know he's the same kind of doctor my dad is, right? That's just too damn weird."

"You're the only person on earth who is not okay with dating a successful and handsome doctor."

"I don't know if I'm ready yet."

"How does one get ready to go on a date? Let's see. I know. I take a shower, put on makeup, fluff my hair, and it's a done deal."

"You know what I mean."

"Actually, I do not know what you mean. You go on dates. You're all secretive about them, but you do go."

"I go on dates with people I choose." He shuffled in his seat.

"Ah, so that's the problem. You like to be the one in charge."

He shrugged. "I like to pursue. It's my preference."

"Has this guy done anything besides text you?"

He rolled his eyes. "He sent flowers. Stalker."

Felicity turned toward Sebastian. "He sent you flowers? That is the sweetest thing ever."

"It's creepy. He's got my home address."

"That he got from the women, I'm assuming?"

"I should never have let them have it. They said they were going to send me a Christmas card."

"What kind of flowers?"

He rolled his eyes. "Yellow roses, you know, because we're just friends right now but there could be more." He stuck out his tongue and put his finger to his mouth like he was gagging.

Felicity let her eyes go big, "Sebastian, I've never seen this catty side of you. I didn't know it existed. This guy must really be getting to you."

"He is not," Sebastian said, biting on his lip.

Felicity could not hold back her grin. "Go out with him.

He clearly is thoughtful, and he's persistent. Those are both good qualities."

Sebastian met her gaze. "Go with me."

"Go on your date with you? Like a chaperone?"

"Like a double date."

"Does he have a straight friend or something?" She lifted an eyebrow, but on the inside, she felt like she was cheating on Scott, which was ridiculous, because she was absolutely not dating him.

"I mean you and Scott."

"Oh," she said, sitting back in her seat. "That's not gonna happen."

"Why not?"

"I pretty much destroyed any chance of him ever wanting to lay eyes on me again last night."

"Last night was the caroling event. What could have gone wrong there?"

She let out an exhausted breath. "After everyone dispersed, he and I went to that hotel in Destin that has the life-size gingerbread house in the lobby."

Sebastian snickered. "That does not sound like you at all."

"I know, but I was thinking it would be a safe place. Kids around, plenty of people. Nothing could happen."

"But I'm guessing something did."

Felicity adjusted her sunglasses. "There was this whole Lovers Lane room. It was really cheesy and stupid."

Sebastian smiled. "Let me guess, there was mistletoe involved."

"How did you know?"

"You said cheesy and it is Christmas time."

She gave him a look.

He covered his mouth with his hand. "That's the cutest thing ever."

"Until I broke away and ran like Caitlyn Jenner."

"Did you text him with an apology or anything?"

She had the good sense to look contrite. "No. Not yet."

"What a perfect way to apologize. You say you're sorry and that you'll treat him to dinner."

"You really think this guy is going to go to dinner with me after what I did?"

"Absolutely he will. He's into you."

"I doubt he is anymore. How about I bring Ashe? He can play straight for a night."

"No way. We can always sniff out our own. Besides, I'm not ready for any of our people to meet this guy yet."

She wiggled in her chair. "Fine, I'll find somebody."

"I need it to be Scott."

"Why?"

"Because I like Scott. I'm comfortable with him. I don't want two newbies to make conversation with."

She stared at her friend, letting the shame and embarrassment of running out on Scott last night consume her. "I don't know, Sebastian."

He put on his serious face. "Do you remember that time back in high school when I took you to the homecoming dance so that you could make Brad Bennington jealous? You said you owed me one for that. I'm cashing in."

"You can't be serious?"

"I'm dead serious. Pay up." He held out a hand for effect.

She put on her best desperate look.

He narrowed his gaze. "Do I need to bring up graduation night when Dylan Reed, captain of the soccer team, said he wanted to take me back to his hotel room so that we could *experiment.*" He put the word in air quotes. "But I was too busy holding back your hair while you puked?"

"Ugh. You're never gonna let me live that down, are you?"

"His calves, Felicity. Think about his calves."

"Dammit," she said, remembering exactly how hot Dylan Reed was, and thinking about the opportunity of a lifetime that Sebastian gave up to care for her. He just smiled at her like he knew he had won.

15

Scott shot off his last email of the day and then leaned back in his chair, stretching, unable to stop the smile from infiltrating his face.

"What's got you in such a good mood?" came Lake's voice from the doorway.

Scott turned and faced him, "That was my last email. I'm done."

"For the day?"

"For the year."

"Bullshit. You can't stay off that computer for three weeks."

"Watch me." He stood up and clapped his cousin's shoulder as he headed toward the staircase.

Lake followed behind him. "How much you wanna bet you'll be on that computer checking email within the hour?"

"I'll have to check email every day. There's no getting around that. But I'm done with my project. Our whole team has been working our asses off so we could get the extra week of vacation before Christmas."

"I can't believe your company closes for two whole weeks at Christmas time."

"Pending email checking," Scott said as he headed toward the kitchen.

"See, this is why I work with my hands. I can't stand the idea of being a slave to a computer."

"And I envy you for that, cousin." Scott said, picking up an apple from a bowl of fruit and crunching into it. He could barely chew from the smile on his face.

Lake narrowed his gaze. "Hang on, you're happy about something other than being done with work. You get off on working."

Scott just kept chewing, staring at Lake with his uncontrollable smile.

"It's that Felicity girl, isn't it?"

Scott waggled his eyebrows.

Lake raised an eyebrow, leaning against the counter. "How is that going?"

"We kissed last night."

Lake frowned. "That's it?"

"That's big."

"Okay," Lake said slowly.

"The Great Wall of China ain't got nothing on this woman."

"Ah, you always did love a challenge."

"She's so different, man. I've dated a lot, and I've never come across anyone like her."

"How do you feel when you're around her?"

Scott thought about it. "Like I miss her even though she's standing right there. It's like I can't get enough of her."

"Sounds like you can't get any of her right now."

"True. But I'm working hard on it. The kiss last night was a big step."

"How did it go? You kissed her and then let her walk inside her house without trying to get in there?"

Scott squinted, thinking about the look on her face when she pulled away from him in that gazebo. She'd been grabbing his hair and pressing her body against him. It'd been even more passionate than their lovemaking had been the weekend of the wedding. It was all he could do to stay on solid ground. "Not exactly."

"Well, give details."

"She might have literally run away from me."

"Now that sounds more like it," Lake said, smiling. Scott just lifted an eyebrow. "Oh shit, really? She actually ran away from you?"

"Oh yeah. Got a rideshare home and everything."

Lake looked confused. "And you're thinking you still have a chance?"

"Big time. Do you think she would have run away from me if she wasn't really into it?"

"Did you scare her off? Come on too strong?"

"That's the thing. She's the one who came on strong and she realized it. She had to stop and physically remove herself from the situation so it didn't get out of hand. If that doesn't tell you that I'm chipping away at the wall, what does?"

Lake cocked his head to the side. "I think you're kind of mental. You know there are other girls out there, right?"

"I like this one." Scott tossed the apple up in the air and caught it, heading out to walk on the beach.

He went straight for the shore, letting the water run over his bare feet. There was nothing like being done with work for the year...except for the woman of his dreams being within his reach.

He should text her—some simple acknowledgment.

Thanks for the caroling? Thanks for the gingerbread house tour? Thanks for the kiss? Want to do it all again? He had to think about it. How about just a simple, *Had a good time last night*. That was it.

"Hey."

Scott turned around at the sound of his cousin Bennett's voice. "What's up?"

Bennett was a buttoned-up, numbers kind of guy. Scott was sure he secretly whacked off to spreadsheets, but Scott couldn't make too much fun of him. He wasn't too far off from that himself with techie stuff.

"Lake said you're done for the year with work."

"News travels fast, I see."

"That's cool," Bennett said, nodding, and staring off at the ocean. It was clear he had something to say, but Bennett wasn't the best communicator of their family.

"You doing okay?" Bennett asked.

Ah, so it was a mental health/mourning check-in. Kind of him, but unnecessary, especially at a moment when Scott was riding high. "I'm doing great."

"Happy to be done with work, huh?"

"Oh yeah."

"Are you still considering carrying on your mom's charity work?"

Scott's chest tightened with guilt. "I do want to do that, definitely."

"Have you put any thought into what that might look like for you?"

Leave it to Bennett to sour his good mood with something Scott legitimately did need to focus on. "Admittedly, no. My job really consumes all my time, to be honest. A ten-hour day is a short one most days."

Bennett nodded as if this were normal. "I hear you. I'm

in the same boat. But we're not getting any younger, and life's zooming by, man."

"No doubt," Scott said, not sure what else to say.

Bennett stared out at the ocean, glanced back at Scott with a forced smile, and then headed back to the house.

Scott eyed him curiously as he headed up the beach, wondering if he should ask Bennett if there was something else on his mind, when his phone dinged. He pulled it out and his heart pounded when he saw Felicity's name. He opened the notification.

If I said I was sorry for running away last night, would you agree to see me again?

He looked heavenward and pumped his fist, apple still in hand. Damn, this was a good day.

∼

SCOTT SPOTTED Felicity and Sebastian huddled close at the outdoor bar in the restaurant where she had told him to meet her. He could only see the back of her head, but her soft, auburn, shoulder-length curls were hard to miss.

Sebastian was the first to spot him. He perked up and nudged Felicity. She turned toward Scott, taking his breath away. She wore a short, black, shimmery dress with long sleeves in a rich, red-rose print and a V-neck that plunged down between her breasts. Her makeup was dark and smoky and her lips were the exact color of the roses on her dress. Scott was sure he'd never seen anyone as beautiful in his life.

Sebastian stood and held out his hand. Scott shook it and Sebastian put his free hand on Scott's forearm. "Bless you for doing this for me."

Scott couldn't help a wave of disappointment. He

thought he was coming here at Felicity's request. She'd said it was going to be a double date, but he didn't know it was a favor.

"No problem. Who's the guy?"

Sebastian rolled his eyes. "It's a set up. I have very little faith that it's going anywhere. That's why I wanted the two of you here."

Scott nodded, but he suspected by the look of nervousness in Sebastian's eyes that he was more excited about this date than he was letting on.

Scott turned to Felicity, who had stood up off the chair and was straightening her dress. "You look nice," Scott said, the understatement of the year.

"Thank you," Felicity replied, clasping her hands in front of her. Sebastian lifted his eyebrow. Felicity gave him a look, and then she pulled Scott in for an awkward hug.

He was not used to her seeming nervous. He didn't know what to make of it.

They stood around in awkward silence for a moment until Felicity said, "What can I get you to drink?" as if they were at her home.

"Whiskey, I guess."

She pointed at him. "Ice?"

"Sure."

She turned to the bartender and ordered a high-end bourbon for him. He didn't have the heart to tell her he was fine with the cheap stuff.

A decent-looking guy with blondish hair walked toward them, his eyes glued to Sebastian. As he approached, everyone got quiet, and then Felicity said, "Flynn, so good to see you."

"You as well, Felicity." He put his gaze on Sebastian. "Hi, Sebastian."

"Hello, Flynn," Sebastian said, and the two just sort of stared at each other.

The bartender handed Felicity Scott's drink and she passed it to him. "Flynn," Felicity said, putting her hand on his shoulder. "I'd like you to meet Scott. He'll be joining us tonight."

Flynn and Scott shook hands. "Nice to meet you," Scott said.

"Likewise," Flynn said. He was almost like a guy from another era with his formal language.

The hostess approached them. "Your table is ready."

Sebastian pulled his wallet out of his back pocket and Felicity dug into her purse. "I'll have your tab transferred."

"Perfect," Felicity said with a smile, and they followed the hostess to a booth inside.

Felicity sat on one side and Flynn on the other. Sebastian stood eyeing the spot next to Felicity. Scott cleared his throat and Sebastian met his gaze. Scott lifted his eyebrow and nodded toward Flynn's side of the booth. Sebastian pursed his lips at Scott, then Scott gave him a smile and slid in next to Felicity. He didn't know who was the most nervous, Sebastian or Felicity. Maybe they were feeding of one another's nervous energy.

The server approached them right away, filling their water glasses and taking drink orders. When he left, they all sat there staring at each other in awkward silence before Felicity said, "Sebastian and I met Flynn the other day at a nursing home in the area. He's a doctor there."

"To be clear, I just do rounds there," Flynn said. "I have a practice in Destin."

"Oh, okay," Felicity said, looking at Sebastian like she was impressed and he should be as well. Sebastian cut his eyes back to her and then took a drink of his water.

"Who were you visiting at the nursing home?" Scott asked looking between Sebastian and Felicity.

"Just some friends," Sebastian said.

"How do you know those three ladies?" Flynn asked.

Sebastian drew a line up his water glass. "I just met them one day over there."

"You were at a caroling event, right?" Felicity asked.

"Mmm-hmm," Sebastian said and then forced a smile. He looked out into the restaurant as if searching for their server. "I should've ordered a double."

Flynn let out a deep breath. "I hate dates." This got everyone's attention. "I never go on them anymore. Well, actually I used to go on them a lot. But to be honest, this is my first date with a man."

Sebastian glanced up at the ceiling. "Lord, have mercy."

"Oh no. I mean, I have been with men. In fact, I've been hooking up with guys since high school. I hook up all the time. Safely, of course. Probably even too safely for some people's taste. I mean, I've been known to use..." He glanced at the three of them, who were each open-mouthed. "Never mind."

Now Scott wanted to know what the hell he was talking about.

Flynn turned to Sebastian. "I've been tested. A lot. Only because I'm a doctor and I have access to these things. I test myself all the time. I can test you if you'd like. Not that I think you need testing." He swallowed hard, peering out into the dining room. "Has anyone seen our server?"

Scott slid his whiskey over to the poor guy, and he took it, downing it. He set the glass on the table, hard. "Thanks, man."

"No problem," Scott said.

Sebastian stood. "I'll be right back."

"I'll go with you," Felicity said, nudging Scott out of the booth. Scott stood up to let her out and then slid back in, taking her spot across from Flynn.

"They're not coming back, are they?" Flynn asked.

"Probably not." Scott smiled to help relax the concerned look on Flynn's face. "I'm kidding. They'll be back. Although, she did run off on me the other night."

"What do you mean?"

"We were at a hotel, the one in Destin that does the gingerbread house?"

"Oh yeah. Sounds neat," Flynn said, loosening the collar on his shirt.

"We had our first kiss. Well, our second first kiss. We kissed before, like a year ago. Anyway, she ran off. Got her own way home and everything."

"Wow. But you're here together now."

"Yeah, she needed me to come on this date with you guys tonight."

Flynn looked defeated. "I don't know what I was thinking. This guy's not interested in me."

"Oh, I think he is."

"Do you know him well?"

"No. I've just been around him a handful of times. But he wouldn't have come here if he didn't want to be here."

"He's not super receptive."

"I think he's got walls up just like Felicity does. It's up to you and me to figure out how to chip away at them."

"You think?"

"I know."

Flynn smiled, looking hopeful.

A minute later, Sebastian and Felicity returned, carrying shots in both hands. Sebastian set them down. "It's essential at this point." They each picked up a shot, clinked their glasses together, and then downed them.

Scott set his glass on the table. "Now that that's done," he leaned in, "What are these extra safety precautions you take?"

Felicity backhanded him with a smile. "We're moving on."

Sebastian looked over at Flynn. "I kind of wanna know myself."

Flynn turned a shade of red Scott hadn't seen even on Valentine's Day.

AN HOUR AND A HALF LATER, they had eaten dinner, drank wine, and agreed to forgo the dessert menu. Sebastian and Flynn were in their own conversation on their side of the booth. Scott leaned in to Felicity. "I think we should let them have the rest of the night to themselves. What do you think?"

Felicity gauged the situation. "I think you're right, even though I'm loving watching Sebastian flirt. I don't ever get to see it. He's so secretive with the guys he dates. He never introduces us."

The server came with the bill in hand. "I'm just gonna leave this right here." All four of them went for it.

"Ladies first," Felicity said, reaching over Scott and grabbing the leather folder. She held it in her hand, grinning triumphantly. Flynn snatched it from her. "Nobody's touching this bill except for me. I'm the new guy and the three of you have put up with my quirks all night. Consider it my penance."

Felicity shrugged, smiling at Sebastian, who was practically beaming.

After the tab was paid, they migrated out to the sidewalk.

"I hope none of us plans on driving after the evening we've had," Sebastian said.

"My family's rental is actually close enough that I was able to walk," Scott said.

"Me too," Felicity said, giving Scott a smile. So she did live right around there. Scott had wondered if that might be why she had been hiding her location from him.

"I'm going to get a rideshare back to Seacrest," Sebastian said, turning to Flynn. "Where are you?"

"WaterSound. I just had a house built there."

"Oh, so you two are close enough to share a ride then," Felicity said.

Sebastian tapped into his phone. "I'll drop you on my way."

They all stood, attempting to hide the knowing grins on their faces.

Sebastian pocketed his phone. "Five minutes away."

"I'll make sure Felicity gets home safely," Scott said.

"That would be great," Sebastian said, giving Felicity a triumphant grin.

She glared at him and then gave Flynn a hug. "Thanks so much for dinner."

"Thanks for coming, all of you," he said, with his gaze landing on Sebastian.

Scott shook Flynn's hand, thanked him, and then turned to Felicity. "To your place?"

She let out a sigh. "To my place."

16

F elicity led Scott through the parking lot to her condo.

"Wow, right on the ocean. You must do pretty well for yourself," Scott said.

"To be fair, this is one of Chase's properties. I'm renting it for a steal."

"Ah, I should've known." His neck went red.

"It's so cute that you're jealous of a happily married man."

"A guy who you slept with multiple times, right before you slept with me, right?"

She shrugged, not wanting to give too much away.

"Was there anyone between him and me?"

"No," she said, throwing him a bone.

"Has there been anyone since me?"

She thought about it a second, wanting to keep some cards to her chest. "Oh yeah, there've been lots of guys, but I've been really super safe. Some would say too safe. But I get tested all the time. Because I'm a doctor. And I can do that. Want me to test you?"

Scott laughed. "That poor guy. I wanted to give him a roll of duct tape so he could tape his own mouth shut."

"I know, right? But really, I think it endeared him to Sebastian."

"Is he the kind of guy Sebastian normally dates?"

She shrugged. "I have no idea. Sebastian never lets us meet his dates."

"Am I like guys you normally date?"

She chewed on her lip. "I don't know. Maybe."

"Tell me about the last guy you dated before me. Or actually, between me last fall and now."

She scratched her eyebrow, and then fumbled in her purse for her keys.

"Has there been anyone since we hooked up last fall?" he asked.

She let out a breath and then pulled her keys out of her purse. "I don't know."

"I'm pretty sure you do know if you slept with somebody. Or I'd hope so." He looked concerned for a second.

"I know."

He lifted his eyebrows. "And?"

She tugged on her ear. "I've been busy this year. I've had a lot going on." He smiled, forcing one on her as well. She pointed her keys at him. "Do not get that smug smile on your face."

"I'm not. I'm just pleasantly surprised."

She looked down at her feet, feeling herself unspooling.

"I've spoiled you for all other men, huh?" She shoved him, and he laughed. "Or were you being faithful to me?"

"I knew I should never have let you know that little tidbit."

"No, you shouldn't have. I'll use this till the day I die."

She shook her head at herself, looking down at the ground.

He took her hand, turning the tides. "You look enchanting tonight."

She gave him a curious look.

"I couldn't think of a better word. None of them do you justice."

She rolled her eyes at him. "Good thing to say, right here on my doorstep."

"I want inside. I'm not going to pretend I'm ambivalent about that. But every time I see you, I can't believe how attracted to you I am. You're completely captivating—every inch of you, from your smooth skin to the way you dress, to the smile you give me when you know you've gotten one up on me." He released her hand and cupped both of her shoulders. "I can't say you're the girl of my dreams because I never dreamed I'd meet anyone like you. But now that I have, I can't go back to the dating pool. You've spoiled me for other women."

She stared at him, her body so flooded with desire she was afraid if she didn't satisfy her need she'd combust right there on 30A.

She stepped away from him and walked to her door, unlocking it. She opened the door and then stood with her back to it, holding it open for him. He sauntered in, holding her gaze, and she knew she was done for.

Once he got inside, she closed the door behind her and took her time locking it while she caught her breath. His hands eased onto her hips, and she closed her eyes, drinking in his touch. He pulled her hair aside and trailed kisses along her neck, throwing her body into orbit. He swiveled her around to face him and went in for his kiss, while her hand went instinctively to the back of his head where she ran her fingers through his hair. It was her go-to move with him.

He slid his hands down to her ass and lifted her onto him. With their bodies still connected in every clothed way possible, he walked the two of them over to the island in the kitchen and set her on it. His hands moved up and down her silhouette and over her breasts. "I love you in this dress, but how do I get you out of it?"

Felicity had never given the L word any consideration when it was spoken during sex, and she had no intention of doing that now. Besides, he was only saying she looked good in the dress. Nothing more.

She twisted around. "There's a zipper back here."

He unzipped her dress and then slid it off of her shoulders. She lifted for him while he pulled the dress out from underneath her, leaving her on the island with nothing on but her bra and thong, which, if she was being honest with herself, she'd carefully selected for the evening.

His eyes traveled over her naked body. "You look even better than I remember."

She inwardly thanked herself for all the desserts and carbs she had missed along with the Yoga/Pilates class she had taken three times a week. She'd done it mostly to have an escape and a way to channel her inner peace through the intensive breathing required for the class. But if it had him looking at her this way, she'd have to make sure to find one down here.

She unbuttoned his shirt, pulling it over his shoulders, sliding her hands over his biceps. She remembered how buff he was, but he seemed to have gotten even bigger than he was last year.

"Thank you for working out," she said.

"You're welcome," he said through a mouthful of her neck.

He unhooked her front clasp bra, cupping both of her breasts, closing his eyes. "Oh yeah. Just as I remembered. Even better than I remembered."

She leaned back, letting him take her breast into his mouth, making her tighten her legs around him. As hot as it was fooling around on the kitchen bar, they had a bedroom right down the hall.

"Bed," she said in a whisper.

"Right away," he said, lifting her onto him and carrying her toward the hall.

"Last bedroom." That was where she kept the condoms.

He dropped her on the bed, and she slid up to the top, ridding herself of her underwear. He undid his pants and let them fall to the floor along with his boxers.

Her heartbeat skittered at the sight of him ready for her. She couldn't believe she was here with him again. She never imagined a world in which the scenario would happen. To her, he was in Nashville and she was in Indianapolis. End of story. Even when she came to Santa Rosa, she'd never dreamed she'd see him down there. But here they were. And how she had put him off this long, she had no clue.

He started to slide onto the bed, and she pointed to the nightstand. "Condoms."

She would leave out the little fact that she had just purchased those earlier today and planted them right there in the drawer. He busted open the box and ripped one off the strip. A moment later, he lowered himself on top of her and kissed her so sweetly it almost brought a tear to her eye. But Felicity was not a crier. Not for something goofy like a kiss.

He pushed inside of her, and she gripped his back. It

wasn't long before they fell into a rhythm, and she wasn't sure how long she was going to last. She had given up on her vibrator not too long after she had come home from the wedding last year. It wasn't doing the trick. All she could think about was him. She found it easier to simply not think about sex at all, as difficult as that was. But this was a beautiful reminder of exactly what she had been missing for the past year and change.

He slowed down, lifting up from her body and kissing her on the mouth as he drove into her with a slower, more controlled effort. The man was full of stamina. He must've been working out extra hard.

"You okay?" he asked in a gentle voice.

"Yes," she whispered, breathing a lot harder than him and he was the one doing all the heavy lifting. "Are you?"

"I'm trying to hold out because I want this to last."

"Don't hold anything back. We've got all night."

"Are you sure?"

"Yes," she breathed, kissing him on the mouth and bracing for impact.

He started up again, this time driving into her faster and harder. It'd been so long since she had come like this. Since him. And the buildup was almost more than she could take. She wailed in response to him and came undone around him. It was another moment before he did the same. She gave him extra credit for his stellar efforts.

He rolled off of the bed and headed to the bathroom. When he came padding back a moment later, she admired his naked frame. She held up a hand. "Wait. Just stand there a second."

He did, putting his hands on his lower hips where those muscles in the shape of arrows leading to his cock bulged, making her mouth water.

"Should I do some poses?" He made a bodybuilder stance, changing to a Hulk move. Though she knew he was joking, he looked damn good, his muscles protruding everywhere from his biceps to his thighs. But he didn't need to know that.

"Get over here, Bruce."

This made him smile. "You know the Hulk's real name."

"He is the most muscled-up guy on earth. But I always preferred his scientist alter ego. Nothing like a hot smart guy." She grinned at him. "I'll have to see if I can find one for myself sometime." He responded to that with tickles to her belly and she squealed with laughter. "Don't, seriously. I am crazy ticklish."

"Oh good. That'll be fun."

"You seem pretty confident that this is going to happen again."

"You better believe it's going to. You said you would be here through Christmas. We've got two more weeks and I just finished my last day at work for the year yesterday."

She lifted her eyebrows. "Seriously? There's three more weeks in the month."

"Yep. My team has been working our asses off for this extra week. We finished our project yesterday. I'll have to check email, but for all intents and purposes, I'm through with the rough stuff, at least until January second."

She considered him. "Do you like your job?"

He shrugged. "Yeah. I'm not gonna lie. I kind of get off on tech stuff." He nodded at her. "What about you? What did you do before you came down here?"

She gave him a look. "What, you're not going to be able to respect me if you know I've always been a full-time server?"

"That's not what I mean. You were secretive about your

job when I asked you about it last year."

She let out a sigh. "That's because I didn't want to talk about work. I was on vacation."

"And now? Are you on vacation?"

She shrugged. "I guess. I'm on a reality break."

"What are you on a break from?"

She readjusted herself, looking for a subject change, coming up short. "I was a pharmaceutical rep for a long time. But a few months before coming down here I had moved into a marketing position with the company."

His eyes went big. "That's not what I was expecting."

"I'm not sure if I should be offended by that."

"No, it actually makes perfect sense. I could see you being a fantastic pharmaceutical rep."

She pursed her lips at him. "Why, because I'm a big flirt?"

He smiled. "I'm sure that doesn't hurt."

"I'm actually very professional at work...most of the time." She gave him a guilty grin.

"How were you liking the marketing job?"

"It was fine. It wasn't really the job that I needed a break from."

"But you quit it anyway?" he asked.

"I just needed away from Indy and my boss didn't want me to work remotely."

"That's weird. Most companies seem all right with that these days."

"You don't know my boss. He's one of these guys who loves to have his team all around him, people hustling and bustling, in-person meetings, he thrives on the energy. I swear, I think he goes in the bathroom and whacks off when we've had a productive meeting."

Scott laughed. "I've known a guy or two like that."

She narrowed her gaze at him. "What did you think I did?"

He shrugged. "I didn't know. I imagined you doing something creative, I guess. And marketing is creative."

"Believe it or not, sales is creative too."

"I guess that's true."

"You've got to come up with ways to make an original pitch. Seem authentic."

"You're absolutely right." He looked like he was searching her eyes.

"What?" she asked.

"Nothing. I was just going to ask you something but then I realized it was inappropriate."

"That's my favorite kind of question."

He smiled. "I was going to ask if you found yourself dating many doctors, but then I didn't want you to think I was insinuating you would sleep with someone for a sale."

"I don't know that I'd go that far. But yes, I've dated quite a few doctors."

"But no marriage material?"

"I've never really been on the hunt for a husband."

"You've never come close?"

She thought about her mom and dad's toxic marriage. "I like to keep things light."

"What's the longest relationship you've ever been in?"

She rolled over on her back. "Don't ask me that. You really don't wanna know the answer."

"What if I do?"

"You think you do. But you're probably just going to analyze my answer."

"I've learned that you make up your own rules. You don't seem to bend to societal norms. Is that fair?"

She shrugged in concession.

"However you answer any question I ask, I run it through the Felicity meter."

She furrowed her brow. "What's the Felicity meter?"

"It's this piece of machinery in my head. It's got all these knobs and gadgets on it. When you say something, I toss it in the machine, and it spits your answer out the other end, cleaning off all the riffraff of what I've always known as typical and putting it in a league of its own minus any expectations."

"Wow. You're as big of a freak as I am."

He smiled at her and she got an intense urge to kiss him, but she didn't want him reading into it.

"So, how long was your longest relationship?"

She eyed him. "There may be other reasons you won't like my answer."

He looked defeated. "It was Chase, wasn't it?"

She winced. "I met him in June, and we remained friends all the way through till he hooked up with Shayla in October. I mean, it wasn't really a relationship, but it was the closest thing I've ever had to one."

"Tell me about it."

"What do you want to know?"

"What made it more like a relationship than anything you've had?"

She thought about the answer. "There wasn't any bull-shit. We were close friends. We talked on the phone a lot. There wasn't all that push and pull—*does he like me or do I like him* nonsense. It was just real."

"Like your relationship with Sebastian?"

"Well, not necessarily. I've never slept with Sebastian."

Scott frowned, and she wanted to kiss his worry lines. "Did you and Chase visit each other during that time?"

"No, but we did have a lot of phone sex."

He put his big hand on her hip, turning her toward him. "See, we could've been doing that this whole past year if you would've taken my calls."

She shrugged, holding back her grin.

"What is phone sex with you like?" he asked.

"I can't tell you here. We've got to be on the phone."

"I'll go in the next room."

"It doesn't work that way. You need the distance. It removes any inhibitions," she said.

"I didn't think you had any inhibitions."

"I don't. But I'm guessing you do."

He gave her a curious look. "Why do you think that?"

"Because you had to create a whole machine in your head to know how to deal with someone who doesn't follow societal norms."

He chuckled. "You've got me there. Maybe you can help me work on that."

She ran her hand down his chest and over his torso. "Maybe we can start now."

"I'm game."

She slid her hand between his thighs. "Tell me one thing you've always wanted to do but haven't asked for."

"Really?"

"Anything you want, within reason. And honestly, even so..."

She could see his wheels turning, probably trying to get up the courage to admit what he wanted. "Can I think about it?"

"Sure," she said, although she had a feeling he already knew but just needed time to admit it. "In the meantime..." She slid her hand underneath him, messing around where she probably shouldn't, feeling him out. She tried to read his facial expression, but he wasn't giving anything away.

She rolled over on top of him, kissing him on the mouth and then making her way down his neck and to his hard, smooth chest. He had a sprinkling of hair, just like she liked. Bare-chested men typically shaved, and she wasn't a fan of the stubble or the vanity.

She kissed and licked her way down to those arrow-shaped muscles, finally finding his cock which had rebounded nicely. She took him in, and he splayed his arms out to the sides, like he was taking in sunshine on a beautiful day.

As she worked her magic, he bit his lip, covering his forehead with one hand. He gripped her arm with the other, which she found somehow more intimate than what she was doing to him. They'd already established during their first go-around last year that he didn't need to warn her when he was good to go. To her, that was the part she was working so hard for. Why would she want to miss out on it? So she reveled in his climax.

He breathed hard as she slid back up his body. As she tried to roll off, he snatched her back to him. She rested on top of his chest, letting herself glimpse for just a moment what a sex life with him would look like long-term. Would they tire of one another? It was hard to imagine that, but it was inevitable, wasn't it? Alternatively, she couldn't imagine herself with anyone else.

"I've been dreaming of that for over a year," he said.

"Did it live up to what you remembered?"

"And then some."

She huffed a laugh.

"No fucking joke," he said. "Not to get weird, but nobody does it like you."

This cracked her up. "I took lessons overseas...in France."

His face turned serious. "Nobody's like you." She shrugged him off, but he was starting to make her neck warm. He put his hand to the side of her face and ran his thumb over her cheekbone. "You're one of a kind."

"You're welcome," she said, with what turned out to be a nervous laugh. Men did not make her nervous.

He furrowed his brow, looking like he was about to say something serious. She moved off of him, glancing at the nightstand. "Oh wow. It's almost eleven."

He let out a sigh, running his hand through his hair. "Right," he said as if in defeat.

"It's just that I've got a big day tomorrow. I'm meeting with Raven early to go over some things for your party, as a matter fact."

He nodded, getting out of bed. "Yep. Got it."

She jumped off of the bed and went to her closet, finding her short, silk robe, her heart thumping in her chest. She needed him out of there before she did or said something stupid.

By the time she had it wrapped around her, he had his pants on and was grabbing for his shirt.

She tried to avoid watching him put it on, because every move of his muscles made her a little less in control of herself.

He turned to her. "You okay?"

She realized she was biting her thumbnail. She pulled it away from her mouth. "Mmm-hmm. All good."

They headed to the front door where he took the knob and then turned to her. "I'm a patient man." He winked at her and then closed the door behind him. She blinked and then let out a huff, realizing for the first time that she might already be in over her head.

17

"Your girlfriend's here," Lake said, tossing Scott a can of beer. Scott wasn't much of a day drinker, but fuck it. He was on vacation. And he was having a damn good day.

He'd been wishing for last night's events to happen for over a year, and damn if Felicity hadn't exceeded every one of his expectations. He'd halfway hoped it wouldn't be as good as what he remembered, because she was no easy get for a long-term relationship. But now that he'd had her, there was no turning back. He was sure about that.

"She's here with that caterer woman, Raven," Lake said. "Should we put shirts on?"

"I'm good," Scott said, putting his hand behind his head.

Lake shrugged. "All right." He collapsed into the chair beside Scott.

A moment later, Aunt Kim walked outside, followed by Felicity and then by Raven. When Felicity looked over at the pool area and saw him, she hesitated, causing Raven, who was typing into her phone, to bump into her back.

When he had Felicity's attention again, Scott held up a

hand in a wave. Felicity nodded at him with a pointed look, then sat at the table with Kim.

"How's that going?" Lake asked.

"Making progress."

"What's your endgame?"

It was a fair question. What exactly did Scott want from Felicity? It was too early to think about a serious commitment with her. He damn sure wouldn't bring up the word *marriage*. Not only would she run for the hills, but he had not fared well in that particular commitment either.

"A chance," he said.

"For?"

"For her to get to know me, I guess. For me to get to know her."

"Fair enough. And then?"

Scott shrugged. "I don't know."

"Your life is in Nashville. Hers is here, right?"

"Actually, I think it's in Indianapolis."

Lake feigned a shiver. "That sounds cold in the wintertime."

"Probably is."

"Could you hack it?"

Scott imagined moving his whole life to Indianapolis where he knew nobody and nothing but that it was cold in the wintertime. He felt an irritation coming on, and he peered at his cousin. "Will you back off? I'm in a good mood."

Lake grinned at him. "Just keeping you on your toes."

Scott kept his eye on Felicity as she worked with his aunt and Raven. Lake put in his earbuds and seemed to have drifted off, which looked relaxing, but there was no way Scott could sleep with Felicity sitting right there, making him crazy with want.

As the women stood up, looking to be saying their good-byes, he held his breath, wondering if she would come say hello. She slid him a glance, but to his disappointment, she followed Raven out the door.

He texted her. *You're not gonna say hi?*

It took her a second to respond, but then finally...

I don't want to seem unprofessional.

Then how about I come say hello to you? Where are you headed?

Some of us have to work.

Tonight?

Yep.

Where?

I know you're not planning on stalking me in my place of business...party crasher.

He grinned. *I've been called worse.* When she didn't respond, he typed, *Can I see you tonight, after work?*

Already asking for a booty call. I should've known.

We can just talk. Get to know each other.

She sent back a rolling eyes emoji.

Or we can have take two of last night. I want to improve upon a few things.

She took her time responding, which made him antsy. Finally, she wrote, *Have you made up your mind?*

He furrowed his brow, trying to think of what she meant, and then he realized, heat seeping up through his neck. He was supposed to be thinking about the one thing he'd always wanted in bed but never asked for.

Scott had always been a confident guy. He'd moved into relationships easily. But he never had to work this hard at it. It was intimidating. She intimidated him. And now she wanted to know his deepest, most intimate desires. It both tantalized him and scared him to death.

He could only play coy so long and then she would call him a chicken...think he was boring, plain vanilla. He had to come up with something.

Meet me tonight and I'll tell you in person.

It took her a minute, and then she responded, *Tempting.*

He breathed a sigh of relief, pondering his next move. Before he could say anything else, she texted again.

I'll think about it.

He sat back, a grin etched upon his face. This woman was keeping him on his toes like nothing he'd ever known. He'd never considered himself a game player, but he was all-in right now. Whatever it took. Because as much as he'd thought about her the past year, being with her in the flesh and experiencing her for more than just a short weekend was even better than he'd imagined. He wasn't about to go back to a boring old life without her.

18

"They want us to find them a karaoke deejay," Raven said as Felicity swept back into the kitchen dropping an empty tray on the counter, ready to load a new one.

"Are you freaking kidding me?"

"No," Raven said, tossing up her hand as she opened the oven with another. After she pulled the pan out and set it on the island, she leaned in close to Felicity. "She just came in here and was like, 'We'd love a karaoke deejay. Do you know any?' And then her husband came in and pulled her back out there."

Felicity shook her head, thinking. "All right, fuck it. We can do this," she said, pulling out her phone.

The party they were working was supposed to have been an intimate gathering. Raven said she would handle it on her own, probably to avoid having to pay Felicity. But Felicity had insisted on being there just in case. She'd told Raven she would come without pay and only stay if they thought she was needed. Turned out they needed a staff of at least five. The two of them had been running around like chickens with their heads cut off all night.

"I'm gonna give this guy a call," Felicity said, and then headed to the small bathroom off the mud room that party-goers hadn't seemed to discover yet. Three calls later, Felicity found a guy who could do it for a guaranteed hundred-dollar tip on top of his normal fee.

She took the moment away from the madness to text Scott, the regret filling her heart as she typed.

It appears that Raven and I bit off more than we could chew tonight. I'm not going to be done until very late, and quite honestly, I'll probably be in no shape to see you or anyone else. But the booty call was a nice thought.

She almost typed a heart emoji, but she stopped herself. She sent the text and was about to pocket her phone when she saw he was typing. She set the phone down and used the restroom, which she'd almost forgotten to do in the madness.

When she finished, she picked up the phone to read his text.

Where is the party?

She wondered for a moment if she should be irritated, but something told her to answer honestly.

On 30A in Dune Allen, near Stinky's Fish Camp.

She waited for another text to come through, but when it didn't appear that he was typing, she pocketed her phone and got back out there. She found the client, confirmed the karaoke cost—which Felicity increased to make sure Raven got her cut—and then headed back to the kitchen. "It's all set," she said, grabbing another tray and starting to head out.

"Wait," Raven said, grabbing her forearm. "Are you serious?"

"Yep. And I confirmed the dollar amount with the client also, darling." She gave Raven an easy smile before heading back out. Felicity heard Raven breathe a thank you as she was walking out of the kitchen and into the living room.

About ten minutes later, Felicity was gathering empty wine glasses when she almost dropped her tray. Scott had walked through the front door and was smiling at people as he glanced around the room, finally catching her gaze. They walked toward one another. "You can't be serious," she said.

"What, you think I'm here for the booty call?"

Felicity raised her eyebrows.

"You sounded like you needed help. I'm here to work."

Felicity wanted to kiss him. "How did you find me?"

"I looked for the house with a bunch of cars and found yours. What do you need me to do?"

Felicity dropped the tension in her shoulders and lifted an eyebrow. "If you were trying to win brownie points, you've succeeded."

He grinned that sneaky grin that she wanted to eat up. He took the tray from her. "I'm guessing these need washing."

"Yes, desperately. We're out of glasses. Have you ever been a bus boy?"

"First job, fourteen years old. Looks like the kitchen is that way." He took the tray from her with a wink and headed off.

RAVEN'S BOYFRIEND Easton loaded the last pan into the back of his car. "I think that's it."

Raven tossed up her hands and then let them fall to her sides. "I don't know what I was thinking. I tried to do that whole party by myself. I don't know what I would've done without y'all."

Felicity waved her off. "She made it out to be a much smaller gathering than what it turned out to be. I think it sort of got away from her."

"It almost got away from us. Thank God Scott showed up when he did," Raven said.

Scott shrugged. "I wasn't doing anything."

"Thanks for coming, man," Easton said, offering a hand for Scott to shake. "I would've been here sooner but I had to close my own bar."

"You got here for the best part," Scott said. "You wouldn't have wanted to miss a drunken rendition of 'YMCA,' right?"

They all four did a laugh/eye roll thing.

"I know I'm all gross, but I've got to give each of you a hug." Raven hugged Felicity and Scott and then fell into Easton's arms.

He held her up. "You gonna make the drive home? We can come get your car tomorrow."

"No, I'm good," she said patting her boyfriend on the chest. "Thank you all. Watch your apps for a money transfer. Scott, I need your handle."

He shook his head. "No way. I was happy to help."

Raven's shoulders sagged. "I'm too tired to argue tonight. I'll get you tomorrow." She held up her hand in a wave and then she and Easton headed to their respective cars.

Scott walked Felicity to her car. "That was seriously amazing, you showing up," she said. "We were drowning."

"I liked it. I see now why you like this kind of work. It's energizing."

"You say that now just because you're stuck behind a computer screen. A few nights of this and you'd be ready to give it all up for building your software apps."

He shrugged. "Probably, but it was a fun experience." He

put both his hands on her shoulders and then eased them down her arms. "I had fun with you tonight."

She laughed. "You're an easy date."

"You have no idea how easy."

She lifted her eyebrows, deciding if she was going to invite him home or not.

He opened her car door. "I'll call you tomorrow," he said, leaving her more disappointed than she wanted to admit.

"That's it? You're just going to send me on my merry way?"

"I want to show you I'm in this for more than a booty call."

She perused him. "Are you sure you're not just worn out from that night of manual labor?"

He shrugged. "I've got stamina. I think you know that about me."

Did she ever. "What if I invited you home for the challenge?"

He let out a hard breath, holding her gaze. "I'd tell you to let me take you out on a real date and invite me home after that."

Holy fuck. He was for real. He wasn't coming home with her. She wasn't sure her pride was ready to take the hit.

She tossed her purse in the passenger seat and then gripped the open door. "That's a shame. I thought I'd try a couple of new moves on you."

He bit his lip. "Hold that thought."

"Till when?"

"When are you off again?"

She pulled out her phone and looked at her calendar. "Thursday night."

He winced. "Three whole days? Fuck."

She shrugged. "You're the one who wants to wait." She stared at him, wondering if he would cave.

He took a step away. "Thursday night it is. I'll pick you up at seven."

She tried to hide her shock. She'd been sure he would give in. "Sounds good. What should I wear?"

"I've never seen you look bad." He smiled at her with those mischievous eyes. Some people have kind eyes or a kind face in general. Scott's face was more mysterious. It was the sleek lines of his cheekbones and jawline. They were pronounced, almost like a superhero's. He had been Shayla's superhero. From what little Felicity knew, he'd rescued her from a very bad man. He was tight-lipped about the story, and she understood why. He was loyal. Just one more reason to like him. But boy, would she like to know the rest of that story.

"See you Thursday," he said.

"See you." She got in the car and shut the door. Three whole days without seeing him. They were here, together in the same place. While she hated being smothered by a man, he was doing the opposite. They had such a finite amount of time there, and he was pursuing her hard. But he was gonna let three days go by without seeing her.

She understood about buildup and anticipation, but she was also a practical person at heart. She could not let him know this was killing her.

She didn't get his game. But whatever it was they were playing, he was winning. Because now, all she could do was count the minutes till Thursday.

19

Scott was lying in bed, letting his phone slide between his fingers and then flipping it over, repeating the action as he stared at the wall. Walking away from Felicity tonight had felt like leaving the secret to life in an unopened box. He kept telling himself he was playing the long game, but damn, it was hard.

He looked at the time on his phone. He wondered if she was asleep yet. He hadn't been lying there long. He didn't know how long it took her to drift off once her head hit the pillow. He could text her, but if he woke her up, he'd feel like a heel.

His phone dinged, and his heart soared as he saw her name.

Thanks again for tonight. You really saved the day. You've kind of got that superhero thing going on, don't you?

He settled in, getting comfortable.

It was my pleasure. I was just lying here wondering how long it usually took you to get to sleep once your head hits the pillow.

That's what you're thinking about me while you're lying in bed?

His grin grew. *Only because I wanted to talk to you. I was afraid to wake you up.*

My phone is on do not disturb after eleven, so you can text me anytime. Don't get offended if I don't answer, though.

Deal. You can text me anytime too.

Are you on do not disturb at nighttime?

No, but I want to be disturbed by you.

You say that now...

He wiggled, adjusting the pillow behind him. *I mean it. You could wake me from a deep sleep and I would love it.*

What if you were dreaming of me?

Ah, now that's a tough one. What were we doing in this dream?

It's your dream. You tell me.

Scott's heartbeat picked up speed. He always considered himself a decent flirter, but the stakes were high with Felicity. She was so cool and confident. He'd been around plenty of confident women, but there was something about her that made him worry that if he said the wrong thing, the uncool thing, he'd lose points in her book and she'd become disinterested. Walking the fine line between keeping her attention and losing her interest was a skill he had not honed yet.

I was probably dreaming about that first night we were together a year ago.

Oh yeah?

You have no idea how many times I've replayed that night over the past year.

Any particular part?

I think about knocking on your door and the pounding of my heart as I waited for you to answer.

It took a minute for the ellipses to show up. He hoped he hadn't sounded too cheesy with the pounding heart thing.

Just as his phone was getting ready to go dim, her message popped up.

You didn't seem very nervous to me.

He breathed a sigh of relief.

You do that to me.

I do what? she texted, all innocently.

You make me nervous.

That's news to me. You seem plenty confident around me.

Smoke and mirrors.

What can I do to ease your nerves?

I wouldn't want you to do anything differently. I like you exactly the way you are.

I think you're full of bull.

He winced. Was he coming off inauthentic? He hesitated, not sure how to respond. She texted again.

A nervous man doesn't touch a woman's body the way you do.

He let out another relieved breath and typed.

You like my touch?

I think you know I do.

What parts do you like best?

The ellipses popped up and then went away a couple of times. He waited impatiently.

You seem to understand my body in a way no one else has been able to figure out.

He would never get the smile off his face. He sank down in the bed further, feeling like a king.

She texted again. *Don't get a big head.*

He thought hard about what he wanted to say next, but he didn't know how to say it. He finally just went for it.

Your skin tastes like my own special flavor of candy.

He sent the text, wincing, squinting at his phone with one eye closed.

It took her a while to respond, but finally, a GIF popped up on his phone of a pinup girl from the sixties moving her hands up her leg.

He grinned and responded with a goofy GIF of a late-night comedian licking a lollipop.

She replied, *What flavor am I?*

He let out a hard breath, feeling movement in his groin. He had to get this response right.

Pure desire with a touch of luxury.

She sent back a smiley face.

He texted back, *What flavor am I?*

Hmm...

He fidgeted with his fingers as he waited.

Pure virility with a touch of machismo.

He laughed. *Really? Machismo?*

Nah. More like pure virility with a touch of indulgence. How's that?

Much better. I wish I could taste you now. He swallowed hard, waiting for her response.

You had your chance.

Did I blow it?

We'll see how Thursday goes.

He couldn't believe how attracted he was to this woman. Everything about her filled him with want, and she wasn't even here with him.

Thursday it is then.

Maybe.

He sent back an emoji with one eyebrow raised. *We're on for the date part for sure though, right?*

That's all I'll promise for now.

Understood.

Sleep tight, Scott.

Just seeing her type his name filled him with warmth.

You too, Ellie.

Save my elf name for late Thursday night, if you make it that far.

He grinned. *Santa's counting the minutes.*

20

When Felicity was eight, selling popcorn for her school's fundraiser, she sold more than any other kid in the entire school. When she was a pharmaceutical rep, she was the youngest person to ever achieve Key Persuader, an award that got her a huge bonus and a trip to Ireland. The year she turned thirty, she trained for and ran the Monumental Half-Marathon, though she'd never been much of a runner until that year.

But the biggest feat of her life? Making it through the past three days without seeing Scott.

To be fair, they'd been texting, a lot. She'd been grossly disappointed with herself for breaking down and texting him that first night, essentially making the first move after he had rejected her and sentenced her to three days without seeing him. But he had taken on the brunt of the pursuing ever since.

She had gotten him on her schedule of sleeping late and going to bed even later. After she'd come home from work the past three nights, he'd somehow known the second her head hit the pillow and jumped into her phone with a text, which subsequently kept them up for hours texting. Or if she was being honest, sexting.

They'd gotten down and dirty in the best possible way, each night digging themselves deeper into the hole of shameless debauchery, both of them too giddy to climb out of it just yet. They filled their time with extravagant indulgences, descriptions of what was to come, and promises of nights of eroticism unmatched by the most lurid and provocative romance novels ever written. Now they had to somehow live up to the talk. She almost felt up for the challenge.

She started off by putting on the sexiest dress she'd ever worn in her life. Many would consider it a slip. It was white silk with spaghetti straps and a neckline that plunged between her braless breasts, which were covered only by some flimsy cups that could easily be torn away and discarded. She only wore those so she wouldn't get arrested for indecent exposure at dinner. This was a family town.

She was going for a wintry white, snowy look, though the mild December weather was providing a breezy sixty-eight-degree night.

She swept her hair up to expose her neck, mainly because Scott had mentioned how sexy it was to him. She was no dummy.

She'd visited her waxing specialist, selected a pale pink for her manicure and pedicure, had her hair blown out and legs elevated with a brand-new pair of sky-high heels to complete the perfect date look.

As the doorbell rang, she pressed lip gloss between her lips with a wink in the mirror and smiled her way to the front door. She pulled it open, bringing an unexpected sight into focus.

"We need you."

All six and a half feet of Chase O'Neil stood in her door-way, threatening to ruin the most anticipated night of her life.

Bo Harrison pushed him inside. "Felicity can talk sense into him. Bring him on in, Blake."

Blake Evans frog-marched a pink-faced Sebastian through the parking lot.

Felicity tossed up both hands, glancing between all these boys. "What is happening?"

"He's blowing off an amazing guy, that's what's happening," Blake said, leading Sebastian into the condo.

"We got any whiskey around here?" Chase asked, opening cabinets.

"Right here," Ryder, Meade's new guy said, bringing up the rear. He set a bottle on the bar while Chase pulled out glasses.

Felicity pinched the bridge of her nose. "Okay, let's take a breath."

Bo seemed to notice Felicity for the first time, looking her up and down. "Damn, look at Fliss. Got a hot date or something?"

"Who's the lucky guy?" Ryder asked.

"There he is," Bo said, looking in the direction of the front door, which was still open.

Felicity turned to find a gorgeously groomed Scott standing there looking at all these men in her living room. This was really not how she wanted to see him for the first time after the anticipation they had built between the two of them during the past three days. She'd wondered if they'd even be able to make it out of the apartment without ripping one another's clothes off. But the wall of men who had infil-trated her living room served as the most inconvenient cock block ever to have lived.

"Come on in, man. Have a drink," Bo said, as if it were his house.

Scott, looking dashing in his coal gray button-down, glanced around like a deer in headlights, finally landing his gaze on Felicity. She walked over to him, pushing him out onto the landing. "I think we stepped into a nightmare. They just showed up. I don't even know where they came from."

He thought about it a second and then his shoulders drop. "I think I know. They were having a guys' happy hour. They invited me but I declined, saying I had other plans. To be fair, I didn't mention you."

Felicity gave him a skeptical look. "Yeah, but they could've put two and two together." She glanced around at the guys inside her house. "Cock blockers."

He took her hand, getting her attention. "You look unfuckingbelievable."

She demurred. "You don't look so bad yourself." She let out a sigh, glancing at the guys again. "How are we gonna get rid of them?"

"They'll get bored and leave eventually. We've waited three days. We can't wait another half hour or so?"

She bit her lip. "Is that a challenge?"

"Maybe so."

She shrugged, looking him up and down. "No problem."

He ran his knuckle up her torso, sending heat to her core. She stepped away from him. "No touching."

"Are these your new rules?"

"For this game."

"No problem," he said, repeating her words.

He walked past her, holding her gaze and leaving her with the cutest little smile she could eat up. He went to the kitchen. "I'll take my whiskey in a glass with ice."

"Not in a shot glass like an eighteen-year-old frat boy?" Bo said, giving Chase a pointed look.

Chase opened the freezer. "I guess I'll forgive you. But a real man drinks his whiskey warm to amplify the burn."

"Maybe we can invite one over to show us how to drink it," Bo said.

Felicity sidled up next to Sebastian. "Really? This is what you've come to? Crashing my date?"

"You know this wasn't my idea."

"I know you could've stopped it."

"I'm a sucker for these boys. I'll do anything they ask me to."

"They are a little irresistible," Felicity said, leaning into Sebastian as they perused their boys.

"Look at your man. Yummy."

"Mmm," Felicity said, salivating a little. She led Sebastian to the balcony. "What's this nonsense about you blowing off your own amazing guy?" She closed the sliding glass door behind them.

Sebastian walked over and gripped the balcony. "I don't know, Felicity. This just isn't me, this whole relationship thing."

"It hasn't been very long. Just a few days."

"I know, but this isn't a casual guy. This is a family man. He wants kids." He pointed at his chest. "Me, a dad? Have you ever heard of anything more ludicrous?"

Felicity squinted, thinking about it. "I actually can't imagine anyone on the planet who would make a better father than you."

He rolled his eyes, rubbing his neck. "You've got to be kidding," he said, glancing out at the ocean. "Like I had any kind of father figure to learn from."

She walked up behind him, putting her arms around his

slight body, resting her cheek on his shoulder. "You love more fiercely than anyone I've ever known."

"My friends, not men, or kids."

"You think you can't grow to love Flynn and your own children the way you love us?"

He covered her arms with his own, squeezing her to him. "It's easy to take care of you guys. You mostly take care of yourselves. My help is ancillary. I don't know how to take care of people I'm a hundred percent responsible for."

She gave him a good squeeze and then stood beside him. "Do you think anyone knows how to do that before they're tossed into the situation?"

He sighed. "I guess not. It just scares me, a lot." He met her gaze, looking more fearful than she'd ever seen him.

She put her hand on his cheek, rubbing her thumb along his cheekbone. "You're such a uniquely special person, Sebastian. You deserve the most amazing love anyone's ever had. You deserve to have children that you care for and want to lay down your life for. My God, I can only imagine the ferocity with which you would love those kids, and Flynn if it goes that direction. That would be the luckiest family on the planet, the one you put together."

He chewed on the inside of his lip. "Change is scary."

"Change is inevitable."

He looked at the ocean again. "Can you imagine me telling my dad I was getting married and having kids?"

"You have no obligations to him. You can feel free to move about your life without his approval."

"I know," Sebastian said, sounding unconvincing.

"Maybe you could use a trip back to Indy to visit him. Sit down with him and have a little chat."

Sebastian shook his head at the rolling shore. "I don't know if I can do it."

"I don't know if you can move forward without doing it," Felicity said.

He inhaled a sharp breath, and she rubbed his back.

The sliding glass door opened and Blake poked his head outside. "Are we making any progress?"

Blake and Sebastian had a uniquely close relationship. They met one another through Cassidy, Blake working for her as a handyman and Sebastian frequenting her bakery every day to bring treats to the ladies at the nursing home. The three of them had formed the core group that grew into this amazing circle of friends. Those three spent Thanksgivings and Christmases together, taking care of each other before there was a bigger group to help with the caretaking. Felicity worried less about Sebastian being down here on his own once she met Blake.

"We're getting there," Felicity said.

"You know I know Flynn, right?" Blake asked, coming outside and closing the door behind him.

Felicity blinked, forgetting Blake was a doctor sometimes. According to Maya, he started out as a handyman, hiding the fact that he was a doctor from everyone. There was certainly a story there. "No, I didn't know that. Have you worked with him?"

"We're both a part of a local charitable organization. He and I worked side-by-side at a Free Clinic Saturday in Panama City about six months ago. After spending the day with him, I wanted to set him up with Sebastian, but I didn't wanna be that guy who sets up the only two gay people he knows just because they're both gay. But I really did think he would be perfect for him."

"I'm in the room," Sebastian said. "You can address me directly."

"I couldn't believe they ended up meeting a different

way," Blake said, ignoring Sebastian and addressing Felicity. "Flynn and I have kept in touch via text, just saying something every once in a while. I texted him and told him I knew Sebastian. Then he dropped by the clinic the other day for a consult and we talked about it some more."

Sebastian tossed up his hands. "So glad this is working out for you, Blake. As long as you're happy that's all that matters."

Felicity pointed at Sebastian. "So this was meant to be, wasn't it?"

Blake just smiled and shrugged.

"Where is that liquor," Sebastian said, pushing past the two of them to the sliding glass door. "I hope one of you is staying sober to drive my ass home."

Blake followed after Sebastian. "Your boy's got your back."

Felicity followed them inside and found an open barstool next to Scott. She slid onto it, stealing his whiskey and taking a drink. She swallowed, the burn infiltrating her throat. "Man, I always forget I don't like whiskey," she said, passing the drink back to him.

"It's a man's drink," Chase said, puffing out his chest holding up his glass.

"How would you know?" Bo said.

Chase just beamed back, always up for being the butt of the joke. He looked at Felicity. "Did you get him squared away?" he asked, nodding at Sebastian.

"He'll come around," Felicity said.

"He's right here," Sebastian said, waving dramatically.

"What about the two of you? What's happening here?" Chase asked, waggling his eyebrows.

"Not much since the group of you arrived," Scott said.

"I'm sorry, are we interrupting something?" Chase asked, attempting to look innocent.

Scott jerked a thumb over his shoulder. "How about you bozos hit the road so my lady and I can start our evening?"

"But we just got here," Chase said. "I haven't even asked Scott about his intentions with my friend here."

Blake took Chase's drink from him. "All right, big guy. The fun's over."

"Aww, fuck. All right then. Y'all need anything before we go? Some fine wine? Candles? A feather boa?"

Scott stood. "Out...now." He still had a hint of a smile to his tone, but he was making it clear that he'd had enough bullshit for the night.

Chase held up his hands. "All right, we're going. Nobody around here is any fun anymore."

Ryder stuck out a hand to Scott. "I know this is bad timing, but I wanted to introduce myself. I'm Ryder. I'm with Felicity's friend Meade. I'm just glad there's another somewhat new guy for them to pick on."

Scott shook his hand. "I think we can hold our own."

Ryder winked at him. "Strength in numbers never hurts."

Felicity stood at the door waving them all out. Once they were rid of all of them, she shut the door and locked it. She turned to Scott shaking her head. "I honestly don't know what that was about."

"Oh, I think you do."

She cocked her head to the side.

"Chase is jealous."

She rolled her eyes. "Don't be ridiculous. He's very happily married."

"He might be, but it's not been that long ago that the two of you were together." He slid his hands over her hips, smoothing the silk against her skin. "He can be jealous all he wants. I'm the one who's here now."

"Those guys didn't rattle you at all?"

He slipped one of the straps off her shoulder. "Uh-uh," he uttered as he traced kisses along her neck.

The other strap came off her other shoulder as well, and the dress skimmed down her body, falling to her feet. She quickly rid herself of the cups that she had lightly glued to her skin, covering her breasts.

He made his way down her chest to her breasts, making her inwardly scream with want.

He hooked his fingers into the sides of her thong and slid it down her legs as he dropped to his knees in front of her.

She wrapped her leg around his neck, holding herself steady against the wall as he made contact with her most sensitive parts. He pulled her other leg over his shoulder, holding her whole weight up as he made her body moan with his tongue. The intensity of the moment and the idea of his strength and capability had her flaming up like gasoline on a fire. She rocked with release, letting out a howl of pleasure as he lived up to all the hype and then some.

He bit her inner thigh playfully as he set her down on the floor. He stood, dropping his pants and coming up with a condom. He slid it onto himself and was blissfully inside of her before she even had the chance to come down from the first high of the night.

She wrapped her legs around his back as he did all the work, pressing her against the wall and pushing into her with a force so powerful she knew she had the potential to come again, which never happened so soon. It was almost like he was building off the same orgasm he'd just given her.

His mouth fused with hers as he kissed her with such

passion, she could feel his want for her all the way to her toes. She didn't know if he had something to prove from all the innuendo of the past three days or if he wanted to stake his claim to her so all the boys who were in there earlier would know what was what. I didn't matter to her. She just knew unequivocally this was the best sex of her life.

"Fuck," she yelled as the buildup inside her hit a crescendo, and she squeezed a handful of his shirt that she was using to hang on for dear life. She felt him letting go inside of her as well as he released his own wail of pleasure.

She slid off of him, settling her hand on the back of his neck and kissing him, slowly and almost...thoughtfully. She kept expecting him to pull away, but their kiss just seemed to become more passion-filled as the minutes passed. He brushed the sweaty hair back from her cheeks smiling at her in between kisses.

"What?" she finally asked.

"I feel bad. You looked like something that came off a page in a magazine, and I pretty much mauled you."

"With my enthusiastic consent."

"Yeah, but I should have taken you out to dinner and poured you expensive wine first."

"You can still do that. Maybe not tonight, but sometime."

"Are you over it tonight?"

"I just think we have better things to do tonight."

He looked down at her bare chest. "Like what?"

"I think we can get creative."

He grinned. "Hell yeah, we can."

21

———

S cott watched Felicity open the French doors to let the salty, night air through. They had already gone two rounds, but if she stood there with her naked ass on display for him like that for much longer, he was getting ready to initiate round three.

She turned to face him. "Is it too cold?"

"We can get under the covers," he said.

She pulled them off the floor and onto the bed, and then joined him. Her cool skin against his was like a mist in the midst of a sweltering summer day.

She cuddled up to him. "I'm not usually a snuggler, so don't be offended if I roll off here in a minute."

"Noted." He cupped his hand over her ass and then ran it down the back of her thigh. She was so petite he could get his big hand around her thigh and in between her legs easily.

She giggled.

"What?" he asked.

She lifted up, looking at him. "Again?"

"Sorry," he said, moving his hand back up to her ass. "I can't get enough of your body."

"I'm not complaining. Just building my strength back up."

"You're tired, aren't you?"

She closed her eyes, resting her cheek on his chest. "Just satiated."

"I don't think I've ever touched a woman's body that was so perfect."

She huffed a laugh. "I spend a lot of money to make it that way."

He moved his hand back over her thigh "Your skin is so smooth."

"You can thank Anna at the spa for that."

"Have you always taken care of your body like this?"

"As far as wax treatments, pedicures, and facials go... pretty much. At least since I got a job and had my own money. Honestly, I never knew that stuff existed before that."

"Your mom didn't do any of that stuff?"

She huffed a humorless laugh. "My mom's never done anything for herself a day in her life."

"Tell me about her," he said, knowing he might be overstepping, but taking a chance.

She took a moment to think about it. "She's very giving. Selfless. Accommodating."

Felicity's words didn't come out admiringly. They were more bland, almost bitter. After a moment of silence, she said, "She's the reason I'll never leave Indy. Just so you know." She still lay on his chest, but she was a million miles away now.

He felt her distance. She was probably trying to think of

a nice way to tell him to leave. He had to act quickly or this was going to go in a very wrong direction.

"My grandfather killed my grandmother." He couldn't believe he'd said it. He'd never have told her that at this stage if he didn't think he had to, but now the toothpaste was out of the tube.

She sat up, frowning at him. "Are you serious?"

He scratched his head, hoping he hadn't bungled this whole thing up. "Yeah, with my mother watching." She covered her mouth, staring at him. He shook his head. "I'm sorry. I don't know why I just laid that on you," he said, knowing exactly why he had.

He needed to make himself vulnerable so she would do the same thing. They'd had plenty of fun—more fun than he'd ever had in his life. But the clock was ticking on the time they had to build something real past the sex. If he didn't start working on those building blocks now, she was going to be out of here at Christmas. She'd said that was her deadline for going home.

"It's fine," she said. "What happened?"

"He used to hit her, a lot. My mom and my aunt would hide behind the bed in their room until it was over."

"Was Kim there too when this happened?"

"Kim was away. I think that had something to do with what my grandfather was so pissed off about that night. My grandma had insisted on sending her to this overnight camp where kids rode horses. Kim loved horses. My grandma had gotten a night job working at a place called Woolworth's to save the money for it. I guess my grandpa was in denial about the whole thing even though he agreed to it. But once my Aunt Kim was gone, my grandpa got bitter about it and let loose on my grandma."

Felicity sat all the way up, cross-legged, on the bed. "He literally beat her to death?"

Felicity's face paled before his eyes. He sat up with her. "Hey, are you okay?"

She nodded quickly, swiping at her eyes. She inhaled a short breath and then held up a hand. "I'm good. I'm sorry." She looked to be shaking it off and then made eye contact with him again. "You were saying?"

"I'm so sorry for bringing this up." He realized he had hit a trigger he didn't know was there.

"It's totally fine." She gave him a serious look. She was sitting there completely naked and exposed to him, the cold wind from the December night blowing into the room, but she seemed completely unfazed by any of it.

He grabbed his shirt off the floor. It was the only piece of clothing to have made it back to the bedroom with them. He wrapped it around her.

She smiled at him. "That's sweet. Thank you."

"You're welcome," he said, looking her in the eye, gauging her. "I hit a nerve, didn't I?"

She furrowed her brow, looking down at the bed. She opened her mouth, but words didn't come out. Finally, she said, "That's my worst fear."

He just waited her out, not sure what exactly to ask.

She swallowed hard. "My father is abusive to my mother. It's been going on since I was a kid. I've worked my whole life to get her away from him. I've never left Indy even though I've desperately wanted to."

"Will you tell me more about why you feel like you can't leave?"

She shook her head. "I feel like as long as I'm nearby, I can be there quickly if she needs me."

"Does she call for your help often?"

Felicity shrugged. "Once in a while. I've had to pick her up from the hospital a couple of times."

"Jesus," he said, his stomach filling with acid. "When was the last time she was hospitalized?"

"It's been a few years. Once I was in high school, and once I was in my late twenties." She attempted a smile. "So of course, that was like, last year."

He knew she was more his age, mid-thirties, but only because they talked about it at the wedding last year. "That sounds traumatic, especially for a teenager."

"I was so used to it. It's been a way of life—fucked up one, I know."

He studied her. "If you could leave Indianapolis, where would you go?"

She rubbed her chin, looking up at the ceiling. "Sebastian moved to Chicago right after high school. He wanted me to come with him, and I desperately wanted to go. It's only about three hours away from Indy, but that was still too far. Anytime I go on vacation, the further I get away from her, the more my anxiety amps up."

"Do you find yourself with anxiety now?"

"She's not with my dad right now, thankfully. But it won't last." She adjusted herself, slipping her arms into the sleeves of his shirt. There was something about her sitting there naked and vulnerable, wearing his shirt, that gave his heart a squeeze like it had never felt before.

"When did they split up?"

"He left her last spring. I thought finally, she's free. I'm free. And then the next thing I know, I meet her for lunch and she's got a black eye." She shook her head, looking at the ceiling. "I knew right then that it was never going to end. My whole life, I thought it was just my dad. If I could only get her away from my dad, that would be it. It would all be over. But she got away from him, and the cycle started with some other asshole. I don't understand how it happens. How can she allow it?" She asked him the question as if he might have answers for her.

He took her hand. "I wish I understood it. I don't. My mom devoted her whole life to domestic abuse survivors."

"Is that how you got involved with Shayla?"

He let out a hard breath. He didn't want to expose anything Shayla wouldn't want told, but Felicity knew, to some extent, what had happened. She'd been at Bo and Maya's wedding when Shayla's abusive ex showed up. Felicity had seen him and Shayla arguing. Felicity was also best friends with Maya, and Maya and Bo knew the whole story, Bo being Shayla's brother. Chances were, Felicity knew most anything he had to say anyway. Still, he'd be careful.

"With my mom's experience and what she's shared with me over the years, I know how to tell the signs. I could see early on what was happening. It was hard watching Shayla's personality turn after she started dating him. She seemed to lose more of herself the closer they got. By the time they moved in together, she was almost a different person. Shayla's a laid-back person. Cool in any situation."

"The coolest," Felicity said with a knowing smile.

"Watching her become skittish and uptight was tough. I knew something was off, and I knew Brian's type too—jealous, aggressive, but charming as fuck. He's just the kind of guy that can slip in and weasel his way into women's hearts and minds."

"I saw that guy. He's good-looking too."

Scott gave her a look.

She held up a hand. "I'm just saying. A good-looking

face will get you a long way." She winked at him. "You should know that."

He shook his head, unable to help a smile even with the conversation they were having.

"When did you know it was time to step in?" she asked.

"I finally asked her about it when I saw a bruise on her arm one day. She blew it off, but her voice was shaky."

"I heard you got a cop friend to come in and hold him off while you moved her out. That was pretty cool of you."

"I felt so guilty...so desperate. It was the least I could do."

She rubbed her hand over his knee. "You're a good guy, aren't you?"

His sense of responsibility fell over him like a wet blanket. "Not as good as I should be."

She gave him a curious look.

"My mom asked me to take over her work with domestic violence survivors."

"Is that something you'd like to do?"

He shrugged. "It's what she wanted me to do. It's what I promised her."

She squinted at him. "You didn't really answer my question."

"Yes, I want to do that someday," he said, hoping he hadn't just told a lie. "I'm just not sure in what capacity. I guess I need to look for a place to volunteer." That was a cop-out statement and he knew it. All he had to do was go to the organization where his mother had worked. He would one day.

He'd just been busy with work, not to mention all the many arrangements with the memory care facility, insurance, clearing out her house and prepping it for sale, and all that came with being the sole heir to her estate. This trip to

Santa Rosa had been the first moment he'd had to take a break and breathe.

"You've had a big year," she said. "You'll know when it's the right time."

He nodded, silently vowing to look into it in the new year. "I want to honor her. It's important," he said, sounding like he was trying to convince himself.

She nudged him. "I still say you're a good guy."

"I'm also a jealous bastard, at least when it comes to you."

"A little jealousy is okay," she said with a smile. "As long as it's not out of hand." She considered him. "I liked the way you stood up to Chase tonight. It was sexy."

He thought about it a minute. "It's tough with Chase, because everybody loves him. And I'll admit he's probably a decent guy at heart. But he still has asshole tendencies. You've got to admit that."

She squinted at Scott. "I'll admit that I think he knew we had a date tonight and that's why he came over when he did."

"Will you admit he wanted to assert that this was his house and he could come up in it anytime he wanted?"

She let out a sigh. "I don't know that Chase is that much of an asshole. I think he's spontaneous and impulsive. I think his life is changing. He's got a baby on the way and he's probably not sure how to handle that." She studied him. "Did you know he had a son who died?"

Scott's heart clenched. "I did not know that. When did this happen?"

"He was married in his twenties and they had a son. He just started talking about it after Bo and Maya's wedding. I think that weekend was pretty profound for Shayla and Chase."

"How did his son die?"

"Chase's mother was driving him somewhere while Chase and his wife were on a date night. They had a car crash and they both died."

"Holy shit."

She nodded. "I know. I think he's probably dealing with a lot of survivor's guilt. Replacement child guilt. I'm not sure exactly what he's going through. But if he wants to barge in and try to cock block us for a few minutes, I think I'll give him some grace."

Scott sank down, running is fingers through his hair. "Fuck. Just when I thought I had a good reason to hate him. Why do you want to make me feel empathy for him?"

Felicity squeezed both of his legs. "Because I know you're a good guy, and I want all my friends to get along."

He lifted an eyebrow. "That's all I am to you, a friend?"

She hiked her leg over his, straddling him. "Friends, lovers, some in-between hybrid, maybe?"

He ran his hands over her shoulders and down her arms. "I want to be more than friends."

"Well, don't be shy there, Romeo."

"I need to be crystal clear."

"What, a good lay wasn't enough?"

He ran his finger across her forehead and over her cheek, tucking her hair behind her ear. "I want an *us*. I wanna know that you're going to take my calls and texts when you get back to Indianapolis. I want to know that you're not going to go on dates and see other guys."

"Like the many dates you went out on when you left me last time?"

"I'm not dating anybody else. I won't date anybody else as long as I have a shot with you."

She just stared at him, a little smile playing at her lips.

"Promise me you won't date anybody else," he said, trying to sound more confident and cocky than desperate.

"I don't know. I had a couple of hits on my Tinder profile earlier today."

He shook his head, looking down at her chest and then back up at her eyes. "You can try to sound blasé, but I know better."

"Oh, you do? What do you think you know?"

"I know I can make you come like no man has ever before."

"Wow. Full of yourself any?"

"Tell me I'm wrong."

She pursed her lips at him, but she did not call him a liar. He knew the chemistry between them was off the charts. It was possible it was just her, and that every man she got together with was privy to feeling like a million bucks in and out of bed. But he chose to believe it was a special connection just between the two of them.

"You're all right," she said with a shrug. She ground herself against him. Her bare flesh on his cock made him instantly hard.

"When was the last time you were with someone?" she asked.

He lifted an eyebrow. "It's been a while."

"Have you been tested since then?"

"I have. All clear."

She bit her lip, looking down at his mouth. "Well, since you were my last and you're clear, that means I'm clear." She rubbed against him some more, sending tingles through his chest.

"You're on the pill, I'm guessing?"

"I'm on birth control."

"I'm game if you are."

She lifted up, guiding him to her. Even though it was their third time this evening, the feel of her flesh on his brought about an entirely new experience that he sank into with pleasure he hadn't known in years. The sex he'd had since her a year ago had been meaningless and with condoms. Now he was skin on skin with the woman he was starting to think could be way more than a fling. He hated to say it, or even think it, but with every passing moment, she felt like *the one*.

He kissed her as she pumped up and down on him. She pulled away, riding him hard, working up and down.

He ran his hands up her silhouette. "I want you to be mine," he said, his voice coming out breathless spurts.

She smiled, and then her face contorted as she grabbed his shoulders. "I'm...yours."

22

"Look at the two of them bonding," Meade said, putting her latte cup to her lips.

Felicity and Meade lounged near the crafts area of the Christmas tree lot while Scott and Ryder examined Christmas trees, talking to the lumberjack who ran the place.

"Scott jumped at the chance to meet up with you guys," Felicity said. "I wasn't sure I could get him out of bed, but turns out all it took was an invite from Ryder."

"I think they're just excited to have one another," Meade said. "The guys in this circle of friends are like a bunch of big brothers in a fraternity. They like to haze."

"They got us the other night," Felicity said. "We were supposed to be going out on a date, and instead we got a cackle of men rolling up on us with a bottle of whiskey." She nudged Meade. "Ryder was carrying the bottle."

Meade shook her head. "He was probably just thrilled to not be their target for a change."

"I hope they haven't been too hard on him," Felicity said.

Meade waved her off. "He loves it. That's how guys show

they like each other—teasing, taunting. It's all very homo-erotic if you ask me."

Felicity waggled her eyebrows and the two of them giggled. Felicity was always conspiratorial with Meade. She was her BFF Maya's older sister, and Felicity had secretly worshipped her as a kid. She'd subtly copied Meade's style from age twelve to sixteen until Meade was off to college. They were now friends in their own right, but Felicity couldn't help having *little sister's best friend* syndrome some-times around Meade. She still saw her as the ultra-cool, uber-hip older sister. Felicity would always see Meade that way.

Meade leaned in. "I'd ask how this was going between the two of you, but I think by the looks on both of your faces, I've got my answer." She slid Felicity a knowing smile. "I knew that night at the wedding there was more to the two of you than one weekend."

"Oh, shut up. You did not," Felicity said, loving the attention.

"I did. The way you two danced cheek to cheek, you looked like a couple who'd been together for a while."

Felicity just held back her grin, taking a sip of her own latte.

"How did he snag you this go-around?" Meade asked. This is why Felicity loved Meade. Of course she would assume Scott was the aggressor and that Felicity was worth pursuing.

"Don't you worry. I made him work for it," Felicity said with a wink.

"Good girl." Meade gauged Felicity. "So it's getting serious?"

Felicity shrugged. "If you had asked me that a few days ago, I would've said no. But things have been...progressing."

"That sounds promising."

Felicity shrugged, losing some of her excitement. "I don't know where it can go, though."

Meade squinted at her. "Does he know about your mom yet?"

"I told him the other night."

"And?"

"And he totally understands. His mother was a huge advocate for domestic abuse survivors. She devoted her whole life to them."

"Wow. That's amazing."

"I know. It's almost an eerie coincidence."

Meade shrugged. "So have you talked about what city the two of you may both reside in if this relationship were to move forward?"

"I think we're both avoiding the topic. But I told him I wasn't leaving my mother, that I never would."

"So he'd have to come to Indy then, right?"

"I couldn't ask that of him. He doesn't know anybody up there. And I'd have to be damn sure he was the one before I brought him up to a place where I don't even wanna be."

"Living arrangements are temporary. Can he work from home?"

"I'm not all together sure. But Indy is just a five-hour drive from Nashville, right?"

"Right." Meade said with a shrug.

Felicity pursed her lips. "So I'm gonna make him drive back-and-forth from Indy to Nashville a few times a month? That doesn't sound fair."

"Life is not fair, and neither is love, my friend."

"True. I'll broach the subject, just to get his thoughts."

"Let me know when you do. But just know, I'm on team Feli-Scott-y."

"Oh, you are so, so bad. I mean really bad."

"This is what happens when you date a nerd, Felicity. I'm corny now."

Felicity squeezed Meade's wrist. "You're precious." Meade gave a cute smile/eye roll. Girl was definitely in love.

The boys walked over. "Ryder is taking me on the boat with him this week for his work."

"Oh, how nice, like a job shadow," Felicity said with a smile.

She expected Scott to blush at his own fangirling over Ryder's career, but instead he turned to Ryder and pointed. "A job shadow. Awesome. I can't wait to see what you do. I always wanted to be a marine biologist."

"To be fair," Felicity said, "I think every kid who ever went to a good aquarium wanted to be one."

"Ryder just had staying power," Meade said, smiling at her man.

"That, or I never grew up," Ryder said. "Take your pick."

"Did you two find trees?" Meade asked.

"Yep. Three of them," Scott said. Ryder and Scott smiled at one another.

"Hang on," Felicity said. You're not bringing a Christmas tree into my home. You know that, right?"

"It's the Christmas season. You don't have any decorations up in there," Scott said.

"That's because it's a rental. I can't imagine Chase would like his floor littered with pine needles, anyway."

Ryder whipped out his phone. "How about I text him and ask?"

Felicity held up a hand. "Don't do that. Next thing you know he'll have hired somebody to come in and decorate the place."

Scott took Felicity's hand. "We could decorate it together.

We could make it all fancy and sophisticated like that one tree we saw that night on the pub crawl."

Oh, this man was tugging so hard at her heartstrings. How could a man as hot as he was be so sentimental? Guys like him were supposed to be easily distracted and onto the next woman. But he wanted her. He made it crystal clear every day. And she was finding it hard to come up with reasons why she didn't want him back.

She let out a deep breath. "Fine."

Ryder held up a hand to Scott for a high five. God, Ryder was nerdy. Cute, but nerdy. Scott indulged him and then the two went back over to the lumberjack.

Meade lifted her eyebrows at Felicity. "I'm sorry to tell you, hon, but that man is in love with you."

Felicity's heart warmed. "It's way too early for that. We've only known each other a few weeks."

"And the weekend last year. He's had a year to ruminate over that weekend with you."

"It doesn't mean he knows me any better for it."

"Love moves fast, my dear."

"You're speaking from experience, I suppose."

Meade nodded.

Felicity let out a sigh, watching Scott and Ryder pick up one of the trees. "I don't know, Meade. I've never felt this way. I don't know what to do with these feelings."

"Girl, I was right there just a few weeks ago. But I'm telling you, the moment I gave in and accepted it, that's when everything fell right into place."

Felicity smiled at her friend, not wanting to sully the perfect moment. But she knew things weren't that simple between her and Scott. Or could they be?

He'd have to move to Indy. That was the only answer. Did he want her that much?

She had to let this play out just a little longer and see. Was this a fling for him? He seemed all-in, but he was on vacation, off work, in a different environment. Was this a fantasy for him, or was it real?

She needed to know, because she was becoming more and more sure of her own feelings with each passing day. And if he wasn't on board the way she was, it was time to bail sooner rather than later.

23

Felicity knew of few places more wonderful than Grayton Beach State Park in December on a weekday. It was a beautiful, sixty-three-degree day filled with sunshine, clear skies, and very few beachgoers other than her and Scott. It was a state park, so rather than the scenery being littered with houses and high-rises, all that rested behind them were sand dunes, and in front of them, the Gulf of Mexico.

They lay on a blanket together, on their sides facing one another.

"The only thing I've ever seen more beautiful than this day is you in that bikini," Scott said.

"You haven't even seen the bikini yet. It's covered with this hoodie."

"Yeah, but I'm imagining it."

"What color is it?"

"It's evergreen on top and brick red on bottom."

"You seriously have me in Christmas colors?"

He shrugged, playing with the string on her hood. "I'm a sucker for the holidays. What can I say?"

"Are you looking forward to the party tomorrow night?"

He frowned. "I am, but I don't want you to be working it. I want you to be there as my guest."

"I would never do that to Raven. She needs me."

"She can't hire someone else for the night?"

"She trusts me. This is a big party for her. She's hoping for a good review from Kim."

"She doesn't have to worry about that. I'll make sure she gets a good review."

"Yeah, but she wants to earn it. She wants Kim to rave to all of her friends about what an amazing party planner she picked."

"But doesn't Raven just handle the catering part? Don't you handle the party planning part?"

"That doesn't matter. I'm just a paid hand. It's Raven's business."

"You're really good at the party planning thing, aren't you?"

She shrugged. "I'm not bad."

"Do you like doing that?"

"Actually, I love it."

"Have you thought about going into business with her?"

She gave him a look. "You know I can't stay here."

He nodded concession. "What's she gonna do when you go back to Indianapolis?"

"Probably kick up her feet. She's been killing herself this Christmas season. She hasn't been letting me work every night with her. She's been doing as much solo as she can because she's so early in her business she's not really in a place to staff up like she wishes she could."

"She probably needs you to hang around till New Year's. Doesn't she have a big party that night?"

"She does have a big New Year's party in Alys Beach.

This couple, Gwendolen and Rob, throw these amazing parties, I'm told. It's a huge coup for Raven's business. But she has no parties between Christmas and New Year's. There's no reason for me to stay around till that night."

"Isn't your rental paid up through the end of the month?"

"It is, but I told my mom I would be home for Christmas."

He tugged on her hoodie string. "Your mom can't come here for Christmas?"

"I asked, trust me." She lifted an eyebrow. "And I asked before you and I were whatever we are now, for the record."

"Whatever we are now, huh?" he said, giving her that look that made her feel scared and excited all at the same time.

"Yes, whatever that is."

"What do you think it is?" he asked, resting his head in his hand.

"No fair, you go first."

"I think we're at the start of something amazing."

She rolled her eyes. "Ah-MAY-zing," she said, emphasizing the middle syllable.

"What's wrong with amazing?"

"It's an overused word. How about good. Solid. Sturdy."

"Okay then, we're at the start of something sturdy."

She hinted at a smile. "Better."

He squeezed her hip. "I might not know what it is, but I know how I feel."

"Oh yeah?" she asked, her voice coming out softer than she meant for it to. She was losing her hard-fought bravado.

"Mmm-hmm," he said, looking at her lips.

She waited, and when he didn't say anything else, she said, "Well, spill it."

"I think you're making me feel things I don't usually feel."

She rolled her eyes. "Oh good. Crystal clear."

He chuckled. "Okay, you're making me feel really solid. How's that?"

"Better."

"How am I making you feel?"

She stared at him, considering, and then she grabbed him by the shirt. "Frustrated."

He chuckled again. "Why?"

"Because this is complicated."

"It doesn't have to be."

"Yes, it does."

"Why?"

"You know why," she said, giving him a significant look.

"You're gonna have to help me out."

She let out a huff of frustration. "We haven't talked about the thing yet."

"What thing?"

"God, Scott. You're not really this obtuse, are you?"

He pressed his lips together and then ran his tongue across the inside of his bottom teeth like she'd seen him do before. He was so unbelievably sexy when he did that. "Are you talking about our proximity to one another?"

"Bingo."

"Ah. Details."

She shoved him playfully. "Not details. I've told you already, I can't move from Indy."

"I heard you."

"And, so?"

"So what?"

"So what does that mean?"

He ran the backs of his fingertips down her chest and to

her stomach, pinching her in the belly, making her flinch. "It means I'm gonna have to move to Indy." He met her gaze, and tingles ran all through her chest.

"You're not serious."

"I'm dead serious."

"You would move to Indianapolis?"

"I would. I will. I just need you to ask."

She let out a huge breath of relieved frustration. "You know I can't ask you to do that."

"Why can't you? I'm asking you to ask me."

"You would give up your whole life in Nashville and move to Indianapolis?"

"In a heartbeat," he said, staring at her so seriously she almost felt her body elevate off the blanket.

"What about your job?"

"I talked to my boss. I told him I was considering a move and that I wanted to know if I could work from home the bulk of the time."

She hated how excited she felt. It was way too desperate, too out of control. "And what did he say?"

"He said okay."

"Seriously?"

He chuckled. "Seriously. He said as long as I could be in Nashville for big meetings, that he would agree to it."

"How many big meetings? How often?"

"Don't you worry about any of that. It wouldn't be much. No more than a couple or three times a month."

She just stared at him, wondering if this was real. "When did you have this conversation with him?"

"Earlier this week."

She shoved him again. "Why didn't you say something?"

"I was afraid you'd think I was moving too fast."

"You are moving too fast."

"Should I slow down?"

She bit her lip. "I don't know. I'm still deciding."

He rolled over onto his back, putting his hands behind his head. "You go ahead and take your time. I'll be waiting right here." He closed his eyes.

She straddled him, sitting on top of him. "You are insane."

"You're the one about to get us arrested at a state park."

They clasped hands holding them up between them. "This is crazy. Completely nuts," she said.

"That's how I've felt since the day I met you."

She shook her head. "I'm calling bullshit. You were in love with another woman the day you met me."

He gazed at her. "Do you remember the day you walked into that Starbucks, and I was sitting there?"

"Vaguely," she said, lying through her teeth.

"It had to have shown on my face, the way I reacted to your presence. It was like I woke up from a deep sleep."

She smiled, wondering how much of it was real and how much was revisionist history. "You did seem a little bit open-mouthed. I just figured you were ga-ga over Shayla. Who wouldn't be?"

"I was experiencing all kinds of feelings. Guilt, protectiveness, friendship, love of someone who I was close to. But when you walked in, it was like a glass of ice water to the face. It felt like a clean slate. Like a rainbow after a hurricane."

She dropped his hands and pressed down on his chest. "Now you're just getting cheesy."

"I never said I knew how to express myself. I just know I've never felt this way around anyone. I never knew feelings like this could exist."

She hiked her leg off of him and lay back down beside

him. He turned to face her, and they just lay there, side-by-side, staring at each other. She put her hand in the middle of them and he took it, kissing her knuckles. "I think you're amazing, Felicity. And I don't care if I'm supposed to use that word or not. It's what you are. There's no better way to describe you."

"I think you're pretty sturdy yourself," she said.

"Invite me to Indianapolis."

She shook her head. "You really are trying to worm your way into my heart, aren't you?"

"With everything I've got."

Heat pulsated through her body. "You'd be ready for this? Ready for a relationship with me?"

"I've never been more ready for anything in my life."

"God, Scott," she said, her voice coming out soft, almost in a whisper, "you make me think of possibilities."

He smiled. "That sounds promising."

"I hope so."

"I know so."

She decided to let the conversation go there, because she didn't think she could possibly float any higher than she soared right at that moment.

24

K im decided at the last minute that she wanted to leave each of the partygoers with a gift bag, so she had sent Scott and Lake out on a wild goose chase for the perfect souvenirs. They'd been to seven different stores, sending pics of each one until she finally decided on the right contents for the bags while she worked on the house.

It was getting close to seven o'clock, when people would start arriving. Scott had planned on seeing Felicity early and even helping her and Raven get set up, but at this rate, he'd be lucky to make it on time.

"Do you know who all is coming down for this?" Scott asked.

Lake rattled off the names of some of their relatives and family friends while the cashier rang them up.

"That many, huh?" Scott said, surprised at the number of people they knew willing to travel for Christmas. But Christmas in Santa Rosa was something to travel for, after all.

Lake gave him a sympathetic look. "So much for it being about you and your mom."

"Oh don't worry about that. I don't ever need it to be about me. Kim's just trying to do her best to make this Christmas good for all of us."

Lake nodded, looking down at the counter, but the furrow in his brow indicated he wasn't completely in agreement.

After they gathered the bags and were heading to the car, Lake said, "How are you doing with all of this? Your first Christmas without your mom?"

"I'm fine. Honestly, she was so sick in the end, it's just a relief that she didn't have to suffer any longer than she did, even if she didn't make it through another Christmas."

Lake hit the clicker on his car door. "What would y'all be doing for Christmas this year if she was here and healthy and all?"

Scott shrugged. "Probably not too much. Spending it with you guys if we could wrangle you," he said, giving Lake a smile as he got into his car.

"You wouldn't be introducing her to Felicity?"

"I would definitely be doing that."

Lake started the car. "This is getting serious, isn't it?"

"Pretty damn serious if you ask me." They pulled out onto Highway 98 and headed back toward 30A.

"Is she on board with moving to Nashville?" Lake asked.

"I think I'm on board to move to Indianapolis." He smiled. "Or Indy, I should say. That's what I need to start calling it. That's what she and her friends who are from there call it."

Lake was silent, so Scott looked over at him. He was chewing his lip.

"Do you think I'm making a mistake?"

Lake seemed to wake up. "No, that's not it at all."

"Then what's wrong?"

He shifted in his seat, putting his elbow on the door frame. "Nothing." He looked over at Scott and gave him a forced smile.

Scott knew something was up, but he also knew Lake was tight-lipped. Scott mimicked his pose, putting his own elbow on the door frame. "All right," he said, touching his forehead with his fingertips, looking out the window.

He knew moving to Indianapolis was a huge decision, and it wasn't one he was taking lightly. But it wasn't like he had to quit his job. He was just leaving his house. He would rent it out. He wasn't stupid. If it crashed and burned with Felicity, he would just move back. It was that simple.

He needed to get used to his family members judging him. They were all on double duty now that his mom was gone and couldn't do the task. That was okay. He was a thirty-five-year-old man, and this was his life, not theirs.

Fuck all that, anyway. It was Christmas. And Felicity was headed back to Indianapolis in two days. He needed to treasure this time with her. He would see her again soon when he got settled up there, but he had things to do.

He'd rent his house furnished, so really all he was going to bring with him were his clothes and a few personal items. He would rent something furnished up there. He'd already looked. He wasn't about to ask Felicity if he could move in with her, and she hadn't asked him, anyway. They would see how it went. He would stay mobile, just in case. But he had a damn good feeling about this, about her. She was the one. He was in love with her. There was no doubt in his mind about that. Everyone else would get on board. They just needed time to let it all play out.

～

PEOPLE HAD ALREADY STARTED to arrive when they got home. As they came through the door and dropped things off in the mudroom as Kim had requested, he caught glances of some of the family members and family friends who had come down from Nashville and a few from Birmingham, but no sign of Felicity. She was probably in the kitchen with Raven.

They'd spent every possible moment together since the night Chase and crew tried to cock block him. On the nights Felicity had to work, they spent those days together. And on the nights she didn't have to work, they spent those together as well. He knew life would be different once they got to Indianapolis and into a mundane groove. He was in vacation mode, and Christmas vacation at that. Still, he'd take the ordinary with Felicity over the extraordinary without her any day.

He snuck up to his room to get changed, splashing a little cologne on his neck. Felicity had commented that she liked it the other day. He'd do anything to make her happy.

When he came down the stairs, he took in the scenery, realizing how fantastic the place looked decked out in even more Christmas decor than Kim had up already. Twinkly lights were draped all throughout the rooms with garland and red flowers—poinsettias, he guessed—and silver ribbons swirled around columns and banisters.

He snuck past the relatives he knew he needed to greet and headed to the kitchen where he found Felicity working side-by-side with Raven, wearing her black catering uniform and her hair pinned back, as if she could ever just blend in.

"Hey," he said, getting her attention.

She turned around, her eyes wide, looking a little frazzled. She moved into a smile. "Hey," she said in a soft voice.

"I'm sorry I wasn't here till now. Kim had us on an errand."

"We heard all about it," Raven said, flashing him a smile over her shoulder. "We totally would've handled that if we would've known in advance."

"Of course," he said. "We found out at like five-thirty. Do you need any help now?"

Raven gave Felicity what looked like a warning glance, and Felicity gave her a knowing look in return. She set down whatever she had in her hand and walked over to him. She straightened the shirt on his shoulders and then grabbed his biceps, giving him a quick kiss. "We're all set. Now get out of here and enjoy the party."

She turned him around and gave him a quick spank on the ass followed by a pinch. How was he supposed to walk out of there straight-faced after that?

Scott greeted his relatives and family friends. Everyone wanted to talk about his mom, which was both nice and a bit stressful. It was like take two of the funeral. Some had stories or memories about her. Others didn't know what to say, so it made things awkward.

Scott really didn't want to be ungracious, but he also was having trouble focusing on the conversations. He wanted to be working side-by-side with Felicity to help make her job easier. Hell, he just wanted to be in her orbit. But he kept his distance and his dignity, being sure to sneak her smiles when he could.

All he really wanted was for this night to be over and to be in her bed. They only had two more nights together, and she was off all day tomorrow, so their plan was to spend the entire day together from the close of this party till she left on Monday morning. The end of this evening couldn't get there soon enough.

As MORE PEOPLE gravitated toward the door, Scott found himself standing near it in hopes of subliminally getting more people out of it. Once the final guests left, Scott was getting ready to head to the kitchen when his cousin Bennett grabbed him. "Got a second?"

"Sure," Scott said, trying to hide his disappointment. They walked to the dining room table where Kim sat, opening a laptop. That was a sight he didn't see every day. "What's up?"

Kim looked up and met his gaze. "Oh sweetie, have a seat."

Scott sat down, and Bennett sat across from him, checking his phone.

"Everything okay?" Scott asked.

"It's great," Bennett said, putting his phone facedown and meeting his mom's gaze. They seemed to exchange a look between the two of them, and then Kim turned to Scott. "Sweetie, Bennett and I have been working on something."

"Okay," Scott said, starting to get a little nervous.

"You know, your mother always wanted to start her own charity."

He frowned, not sure what she was talking about.

"She didn't mind that group she worked with for years, but there were a lot of things she said she would do differently if she were running the show."

Scott just nodded, wondering where this was going.

Kim and Bennett gave each other an encouraging look and then Bennett nodded at Scott. Kim turned back to Scott, and said, "So we started one."

Scott sat back in his chair, gauging the two of them. "Wow. You started a charity?"

"Yep," Kim said, looking practically giddy.

"It's no joke, man. Mom nailed down some serious donors. She's been working so hard." Bennett took his mother's hand and squeezed it. "I'm so proud of her."

Kim waved him off, but Scott could tell she was indulging herself in her son's adoration. "I just wanted to find a way to honor her the best way I knew how."

"That's wonderful, Aunt Kim. I can't thank you enough," Scott said.

Kim and Bennett exchanged another one of those looks that were starting to work Scott's nerves.

"There is one way you can thank us," Kim said.

"Okay," Scott said.

"Come work there with us."

Scott told himself to remain calm, but his anxiety started to creep up. "Doing what?"

"We were hoping you would want to run it," Bennett said.

"Me?" Scott asked, actually pointing to his own chest.

Kim giggled. "Yes you. Of course, you. Who would be better to carry on Diane's legacy than her only son? You know more about helping these survivors than anyone."

"That's definitely not true," Scott said, crossing his arms over his chest.

"You know a lot," Kim said.

"I don't know, guys. I know I'm off work right now, but this is an exception. I usually put in at least ten hours a day. I'm simply not that available."

"We're not talking about this being a part-time job," Kim said.

"We would pay you what you're making now," Bennett said.

Scott almost laughed. "You couldn't pay someone working at a charity what I make."

"Wanna bet?" Bennett said.

"Let me rephrase," Scott said, hearing his tone getting sterner. "I wouldn't allow you to pay me what I make now."

"This isn't about money," Kim said. "This is about helping the women your mother was helping."

Scott's chest tightened. Now he felt accused of being money hungry.

Bennett and Kim exchanged a concerned glance. "Look," Bennett said, "we thought you'd be really excited about this. I asked you just a couple of weeks ago if you still wanted to carry on your mother's work, and you said—"

"I know what I said." Scott recalled his conversation with Bennett that day on the beach when he had just finished work. He willed himself to calm down. "I'm just shocked."

"This is a chance for you to do real good with your life," Kim said.

Scott felt cut off at the knees.

"Not that his job at the tech company isn't good," Bennett said, raising an eyebrow at his mother.

"Of course not, honey. I didn't mean that."

But Scott knew she absolutely meant it. And the worst of it was that it was true. He wasn't helping anyone at the tech company. But he would be at this job. He'd be devoting his whole life to it...to what he'd promised his mom he'd do once she'd passed.

"Is this something I can do remotely?" Scott asked, knowing the answer.

"Well, no," Kim said. "The space we're looking at is on Dickerson Pike in East Nashville."

"Dickerson Pike?" Scott asked, familiar with the area, which was run down and dilapidated.

"We need to be accessible for people who need us," Kim said.

"Of course," Scott said, rubbing his forehead.

"Women will walk in off the street," she said. "Often when women make a decision to get help, it's not like they can make an appointment. They need to be able to go somewhere right then nearby."

Scott knew that.

"They need someone they can feel safe with," Bennett said. "That's why mom will be there with you."

"You're going to go to work every day on Dickerson Pike?" Scott asked.

"I'm devoted to this, honey. I know it's a huge undertaking, but I'm ready to do it."

Scott nodded, his mind swirling. Just a few minutes ago, his biggest concern was how quickly he could get into bed with Felicity, and now he was being presented with an undertaking he never dreamed of.

"When do you need an answer?" Scott asked.

Bennett and his mom both looked taken off guard. "As soon as possible, I guess," Bennett said.

Kim turned to Bennett. "I knew we should've brought him in on this earlier."

"Why didn't you, by the way?" Scott asked.

"You've been hard to reach these past few months, to be honest," Bennett said, giving him a pointed look.

Scott recalled all the phone calls and texts he'd gotten from Bennett over the past few months that he'd given short replies to or never returned. Bennett had always been a caretaker, and Scott figured he was just trying to make sure Scott was doing okay after the death of his mother.

"You've been working so hard." Kim squeezed Scott's arm. "We didn't want to overwhelm you. We wanted to give you time to mourn your mother."

"We knew if we brought you in, you would feel responsible and take on the challenge of setting everything up on top of doing your other job," Bennett said. "We wanted to present you with this knowing you could leave that job and start this one with a clean break."

While Scott appreciated his aunt and his cousin looking out for him, he didn't like his life being planned for him behind his back.

"Do you remember when we were planning the funeral how I said I wanted to carry on her work and you said you'd planned to do that as well?" Kim asked.

Scott did not remember that, or maybe he did. Who knew? He'd been in deep mourning for his mother. He'd said a lot of things.

He nodded and stood up from the table, and Kim and Bennett followed suit. Scott ran his hand through his hair. "Thanks for all this. I'll put some deep thought into it."

"Okay," Bennett said. "That's all we can ask."

The two of them headed for the living room, and Scott just stood there feeling lost. He needed an anchor...something to stop the runaway ship. Felicity.

He walked into the kitchen and found her standing with Raven, the two of them with serious expressions on their faces, Raven with her hand on Felicity's shoulder. Raven dropped her hand, and the two of them busied themselves. Fuck, she'd heard everything.

"Hey," he said.

She turned to him. "Hey," she said, her tone completely different than it had been earlier that night.

He walked over to her and put his hand on her back, but

she wiggled away from him. "We've still got a lot of work here. I'm going to be a while. Why don't you head on in with your family and recap the night?"

"I want to help."

"I'd really rather you not," Raven said. "The optics are bad."

Felicity turned away from him, and he stood there, knowing everything was about to change and feeling powerless to do anything about it.

HALF AN HOUR LATER, when Scott saw Raven and Felicity taking stuff to their cars, he went into the kitchen to help. They didn't argue as he carried a load and put it in the back of Raven's SUV.

She closed the hatch. "That should be it. I'm going to say goodbye to your aunt," she said, leaving Scott and Felicity at her car by themselves.

Felicity looked down at the ground. "I think you should take it."

He reached for her hand, "Felicity."

She jerked her hand away "I'm serious. It sounds amazing. It was meant for you. Think of all those people you can help. This will give your life purpose."

"My life has purpose," he said, staring at her intently.

She shook her head, unable to look at him. "I'm not purpose for your life. I'm a distraction. This is what you're meant to do, Scott. This is what you need to do."

"I just told them I was going to think about it because I couldn't say no right there on the spot. But I'm coming to Indianapolis."

"No, you're not. I don't want you to come."

A knife sliced through his heart. "You wanted me to come earlier today."

"Earlier today I was living in some kind of far out dream. I'm in reality now. This has been fun, a vacation. The vacation's over. We're over." She walked to the driver's side of the car and got in before he could think of what to say next.

As she backed out and pulled away, his heart sank into his gut. She was going to be gone. He was never gonna see her again. She wouldn't take his calls or texts. He was facing the same loss he'd dealt with last year with regard to her. He couldn't believe just an hour ago he was riding on cloud nine and now that was all over. It'd been a dream, a surreal one. But he'd woken up, and now he was facing reality.

25

Once Felicity got her bearings, the first thing she did was text Sebastian. He was planning to ride home with her on Monday. He would then get a flight back to 30A once he hashed things out with his dad after Christmas. But now, she was ready to go a day early. She knew he'd much rather fly, but he was being kind by offering to keep her company while she drove the long haul back to Indy.

Something has developed. I need to leave a day early. So you're off the hook.

Instead of getting a text back, her phone rang.

"What development, sweetie?" Sebastian asked before Felicity could even say hello.

She let out a sigh and then unloaded her burden. She told Sebastian what she had overheard. She let him know how important the work was to Scott and how he wanted to honor his mother. She told him how there was no way she could mess this up, especially them being so early in their relationship.

"Oh sweetie. I'm so sorry," he said. And the fact that he didn't immediately try to talk her out of it made her feel ten times worse. He didn't, because he shouldn't. She was doing the right thing. That was the kick in the ass.

"So are you okay to fly?" she asked.

"I'm okay to leave tomorrow if you are."

"Really?" A huge relief washed over her. She still did want his company, desperately. That way she wouldn't drive off a bridge into a lake. She shouldn't even think things like that, and of course she wasn't that desperate. But that's how she felt at the moment—like someone had ripped her heart from her chest and run it through a paper shredder.

SHE PACKED that night and picked Sebastian up at seven a.m. He was waiting with his small suitcase and a bag of pastries and teas from Seaside Sweets. She recognized the white paper bag with the aqua and pink logo. Her stomach growled in response.

He slid into the front seat. "We're a motley crew today, aren't we?"

"How are you feeling about your chat with your dad?" she asked.

"Anxious. I was actually glad you wanted to leave a day early. I'm ready to get on up there."

"Does he know you're coming?"

"I had to tell him. For all I know they travel to the Swiss Alps for Christmas. I don't even know him anymore."

She put the car in gear. "How did that conversation go?"

"It was just a text, me asking if he was going to be in town for Christmas, him saying yes, and me setting a date and time for lunch."

"Wow," she said, glancing at him and then putting her eyes back on the road.

They rode in silence for a minute, and then he said, "He did end the text with, 'Will be good to see you.'" He rolled his eyes.

"That's something," she said.

"What about you?" he asked. "Do things look any better in the daylight?"

"Not really."

"You know, this really is his decision to make."

She chewed on the inside of her lip. "I can make it easier for him, though."

"Honey, if he decides not to take that job and come to Indy with you instead, that's his prerogative."

The hope was just enough to stab her in the gut. "I'll say no if he tries to do that. He needs to do this, in his mother's honor."

"Understood," Sebastian said, taking a pastry out of the bag and handing it to her by the little paper. "Will sugar help?"

"Is that one of Cassidy's cinnamon rolls?"

"You know it is."

She took it. "FML."

~

FELICITY'S MOM was as excited to see Sebastian as she was to see Felicity. If Felicity was being honest with herself, she was happier to see Sebastian. That was okay. He made people happy, plain and simple.

She'd not gone all out, but she had decorated the house for Christmas with a few things, including a nice artificial Christmas tree. Felicity spotted a few of the ornaments they had when she was a child. There weren't too many of those. They weren't traditional Christmas people who picked out yearly ornaments by any stretch, but it warmed her heart that her mom had hung onto the few that they did have.

"Sebastian, I hope you don't mind sleeping on the couch," Felicity's mom said. "I've already got it made up since I knew you guys would be getting home so late."

"Oh, that's no problem at all, Mrs. Haley. I appreciate you letting me stay here."

She cleared her throat, touching her neck. "Actually, I have gone back to my maiden name. But regardless, you can always call me Rebecca."

Sebastian and Felicity exchanged a look.

"You changed your name?" Felicity asked, so shocked she wanted to make sure she had it correct.

"That's right," her mom said, chin lifted. "Have a seat here at the kitchen table. I know you're both exhausted, but I've made some hot cider. I got the recipe from my friend, Judy. She'll be joining us for Christmas dinner tomorrow."

There was something about the way she said the woman's name that gave Felicity pause. As her mom turned around to walk to the stove, Sebastian lifted an eyebrow. He must've gotten the same vibe.

"It smells amazing," Sebastian said. "I was hoping that wasn't just a candle we were smelling."

Her mother dished out three mugs that were already waiting by the stove. She brought them over and sat them down on the table in front of them.

"Is Judy a new friend?" Felicity asked, treading lightly.

Her mother took a seat. "We've met recently, but she's one of those people who's really easy to get along with." She smiled at Felicity, her cheeks going pink, and then took a drink.

"Where did you meet her?" Felicity asked.

Her mom furrowed her brow, looking down at her mug. "A group at the church."

Felicity felt her eyes going big. "Church?" Her dad had thought church was ridiculous and the whole family had been forbidden to go.

"I started going. This one up the street on Clover. Not for services or anything. Just a group that they host on Wednesday nights."

"A group?" Felicity asked, dying for more information.

Her mother waved her off. "Just a bunch of women chitchatting. Anyway, tell me all about Florida. How was it? Or shall I say how is it? Are you going back?"

"No, I told you I was only there on vacation. I'm home for good now," Felicity said, reaching over and squeezing her mom's arm.

"Well, I hope you didn't come back for me. I've got every-thing fully under control here."

Felicity felt a bit dissed. "Okay," she said, sounding defensive.

"What about the catering company? Have you given any more thought to partnering with that young girl?" her mom asked.

"No, I'm here. You're here."

"Well, you don't have to be here," her mother said, giving her a pointed look.

Sebastian stood. "I'm going to use the restroom." He headed off. Once the bathroom door shut, Felicity's mother leaned in. "You can go ahead and quit worrying about me. I'm fine."

"I thought you were 'fine' after Dad left?" she said, putting air quotes around the word.

She sat back. "That's over. I'm not with any men

anymore. And you will be happy to know that your dad came home three weeks ago and I told him to leave."

Felicity almost fell out of her chair. "Are you serious?"

"Yes, I'm serious."

"And he did it?"

She shrugged. "It took some coercing, but yeah, he left."

"Are you okay? Did he hurt you?"

"No," she said and then put her coffee cup to her lips. "Judy was here."

Felicity leaned in conspiratorially. "Mom, is Judy your girlfriend?"

Her mother swallowed her sip and waved Felicity off. "You're so dramatic."

"Is she?" Felicity couldn't hold back her smile, because her mother was not denying it.

"We are friends. We support one another."

Felicity thought about the group at the church. "Mom, is this group where you met Judy a support group?" Felicity's mom had never even dreamed of going to a support group. Felicity had asked her to a million times, but she wouldn't have it. She always downplayed the abuse, blew it off like it was no big deal.

"If you have to put a label on it, you can call it that. But I see it as just meeting some new friends."

"You go to a support group," Felicity said, unable to believe her own words.

Her mother rolled her eyes. "I was bored. You were gone. I had to make some new friends somehow."

"When did you start this?"

"Back in October. A week or so after you left."

"But you were still with Pete then."

"If you must know, your leaving was the best thing that ever happened to me."

"Really?" Felicity asked.

"Really. It was like a wakeup call. You've always been here for me, and I've never really thought about you leaving. Not for good. But then when you got a job down there, I knew you weren't coming back anytime soon. I figured I better find another friend."

"So you went to a support group when you were still with Pete?"

"I did. The first session was weird and I felt like I didn't belong there. I felt like an imposter. But then Judy asked me to go to coffee, and we went and shut the shop down." She shrugged. "Then we went and had a glass of wine."

"Mom," Felicity said, "you're beaming."

"Quit it," she said, blushing again, and then giggling as she went to take another sip.

"So you and Judy are a couple."

"I don't know how to describe it. We're good friends. But then sometimes we...hug."

"I hug my friends every time I see them."

"Maybe I should say...cuddle. Like when we're watching television together. And we held hands in the movie theater the other night."

Felicity could not stop smiling. "Mom, you are in a lesbian relationship."

Her mother giggled again. "Stop it with all that."

"What else would you call this? You're not just friends. Friends don't cuddle."

"There's no need to label it. Judy is just someone I like being with."

"And spending Christmas with." Felicity raised her eyebrows in a significant manner.

"And with you and Sebastian."

"Does she have kids?"

"She does, but her son is in the Navy and he's stationed overseas right now, so he's not going to make it home for Christmas."

"That's too bad. How old is he?"

"Twenty-two, I believe?"

Felicity frowned. "How old is Judy?"

"She's close to my age. She had her son late in life."

Felicity slapped her hand down on the table, practically jubilant. "Well, this is an exciting turn of events."

Her mother shrugged and smiled, sipping from her mug.

"So, what happened that night when Dad came over?" Felicity asked.

"Judy pulled her gun out of her purse."

Felicity almost spewed her cider out of her mouth. She swallowed it down. "Are you serious?"

"I'm dead serious. She packs heat."

"That is amazing," Felicity said, almost giddy.

Her mom shrugged. "It's kind of hot."

Felicity grinned. "No doubt."

Sebastian came out of the bathroom, gauging the situation, and once he saw smiles, he said, "What did I miss?"

"My mom is a lesbian."

Sebastian tossed up his hands. "Welcome to the family."

THE THREE OF them talked a little while longer and then Felicity's mom got a call that lit her up like a Christmas tree. "I've got to take this. I'll see you in the morning. We'll have breakfast. Judy showed me this great place."

Her mother practically skipped to her bedroom, leaving Felicity and Sebastian at the kitchen table.

"I'll just bet she did," Sebastian said with a wink.

"I can't believe this," Felicity said, staring at Sebastian in awe. "Who would've ever dreamed of it? My mom is in love with a woman."

"Oh sweetie, I don't know who I'm happier for, her or you."

"Why are you happy for me?"

"Because you're mobile now. Even if he can't move to Indy, you can move to Nashville."

"Oh no. I'm not about to do that."

"What are you talking about? It would solve everything."

She sat back in her chair. "No way. That would go over really smoothly. 'I know I dumped you on your ass last night, but never mind. I'm moving in!' Not happening."

"You just need to explain what changed your need to stay in Indy. You're free now."

"It's more than that. There's nothing for me in Nashville."

Sebastian seemed to gain understanding. "But there is something for you in Santa Rosa."

She gave him a meaningful look.

"Got it. Now you're the one with the decision—follow the love of your life or join a new business venture that you're damn good at, by the way."

She shrugged and then put both hands around the mug in front of her.

"This is a tough quandary," he said.

"Ya think? But like you said, he's got a decision to make too."

"True. But it might be nice if he had this piece of information to make the decision with."

She pointed at the table for emphasis. "I want him to make this decision without this piece of information."

"Look at you, putting our boy to a test."

"This time away from one another will be good. We were in a vacation wonderland. We spent all this hardcore time together, but now we're both getting back to our real worlds. Let's see what he thinks after he's had a little time away from me."

"And what you think."

She shrugged concession, but she knew she was all-in. She'd never felt like this for anyone before. She was not just in love with him, she was madly in love with him. And she didn't want to be with him if he was anything less than crazy in love with her.

"Let's go to bed," she said.

"Agreed."

"Tomorrow, we'll have breakfast with Judy, plan the perfect Christmas dinner, and then we'll get you squared away with your dad."

"I wouldn't hold my breath for that one," Sebastian said, and she sensed the hurt reverberating off of him already.

She brought him in for a hug. "All you can do is try." She pulled away from him, holding his arms. "No matter what happens, your family's right here. You know that."

He got teary-eyed. "I do."

She gave him a big kiss on the cheek, and then they headed to their separate sleeping places.

26

Typically, when Scott returned home from vacation, there was a sense of order being restored. Even on the trip home, he was typically ready to be done with the beach and to get back to reality, recounting all the things he needed to do, including get back into his normal workout routine, do his regular food prep for the week, and handle all the household stuff that got put on pause while he was gone. As much as he liked being away, he savored coming back just as much.

But this time, nothing felt right. He'd spent Christmas with his family. They'd gone through the motions, opening the gifts which were plentiful, eating all the wonderful food, and drinking all the expensive wine. But his heart had gone to Indianapolis without him.

Felicity had told him that she only had till Christmas. He'd believed her, but he'd held out hope that he could keep her for one more week and they could ring in the new year together. He was halfway hoping she'd invite him home with her. He could have met her mother, and they could have apartment shopped for him. But now, rather than finding himself with her, he sat on a barstool at EXIT/IN in Nashville, celebrating Lake's birthday.

Lake had been blessed with a December thirtieth birthday, and it had become a tradition to celebrate it in a big way —the unofficial kick off to New Year's Eve. No matter what band was playing at the venue that night, everyone gathered for Lake's birthday. It had become a reunion of sorts with high school friends, college friends—not only of Lake's, but of all Scott's cousins—and some of Scott's own friends and acquaintances. It'd turned into quite the gathering. He would've loved to have shown off Felicity at it.

His cousin clapped him on the shoulder, wearing a cardboard hat covered in silver sparkly stuff. "Happy New Year, man."

"Tomorrow's Happy New Year. Today's happy birthday... to you."

Lake waved him off. "It's just an excuse to celebrate. Flimsy one at that."

Scott shrugged, taking a drink of his beer.

Lake took a seat next to him at the bar. "Have you talked to her this week?"

Scott didn't have to ask who. "I texted her on Christmas Day and told her I hoped she and her mom had a merry Christmas."

"Did she reply?"

"She said she wished me and my family the same."

"Is that where the conversation ended?"

"I asked her some other insignificant thing to keep it going, but she never replied."

"And you just let it end there. You must not be that into her."

Scott slid him a glare. "I fucking love her, man." He wouldn't have said it if he wasn't five beers in.

"Then go after her. What are you doing here?"

He let out a sigh and then pointed randomly into the room. "Go, enjoy your birthday. Leave me here to drown in these suds." He was going for humor, but he came off pathetic instead.

"I know what the problem is," Lake said.

"Oh you do?" Sarcasm dripped off Scott's tongue.

"Yeah. You think you've got to take that job."

Scott rolled his eyes. "Of course I've got to take the damn job. They created the whole organization for me to run it."

"Without consulting you."

Scott sneered at Lake. "Did you know about it?"

"I found out a couple of days before the party. They kept it from me. They know you and I are tight."

"Why do you think they were keeping it such a bloody secret?"

"Because I think they were afraid you would say no and tell them to quit doing it on your behalf."

"They shouldn't have done it on my behalf." He thought about it and then shook his head. "Fuck that. They were right. I told my mom I would take over her life's work. But I've proved to be all talk. At least Bennett and Kim were actually making a move in that direction."

Lake just watched him, looking like he was feeling sorry for him. Scott probably appeared as pathetic as he felt.

"First of all, I can't give her the grandbaby she wanted, then next, I won't even help people who are in desperate situations to honor her legacy. The woman gives me life but I can't give her jack shit."

"Dude, what about you?"

Scott frowned. "Hmm?"

"When's the last time you've done something for yourself?"

"I've done plenty for myself these past few weeks. I've been indulging in Felicity like a bank robber rolling around in stolen cash."

Lake smiled. "And you've deserved it. I've watched you care for your mom for the past few years now. Yes, my mom has helped, but you've been the one dealing with everything —the nursing home, the money, her whole house full of shit."

"You helped me with that."

"Yeah, but you dealt with it all—the social security stuff, the insurance, the grief. When were you supposed to have started this new career of public service? Not to mention you probably spent God knows how much of your own money through all of this. I know your mom lived modestly."

Scott just shrugged. His family didn't need to know about his mother's debt issues, though he figured they all had their suspicions.

"It takes not only time to deal with all that shit, but money. How were you supposed to deal with all that if you gave up your high-salaried job to do some charity work in the name of your mom's legacy?"

Scott thought about it, opening his mouth to reply with something, but Lake cut him off.

"I'm saying, if it were me, I wouldn't let two people tell me what I was going to be doing for my job, even if they were two people I love more than anything in the world."

Scott tried to blink Lake into focus, not because he was that drunk, but because he was trying to understand exactly what he was saying. "So you think I need to tell them I'm not taking the job?"

"Exactly."

"Just like that."

Lake shrugged. "Just like that."

Scott narrowed his gaze. "It must be nice to be you."

"What's that supposed to mean?" Lake said with a chuckle.

"It means you do whatever the hell you want, consequences be damned."

"Pretty much. If you think for one second if I was put in this same situation that I would be staying here for the job and not following the girl of my dreams, you're out of your mind. Look, cousin, this is not your problem. This is their problem. They came up with this place."

"Like I'm really gonna let your mom go to work on Dickerson Pike without me being there in case something happens."

"My mom isn't gonna do this job," Lake said, glancing around.

"What do you mean?"

"I mean this is her project of the moment. You know how scattered she is. She'll try this for a little while, see how hard it is, and then she'll be right back onto her next project."

Scott didn't realize Lake understood his own mom that well. He'd never talked about her like that, but it damn sure did describe her. "Does Bennett share your same opinion of your mom?"

"This is what Bennett does. He gets excited about things and jumps the gun. He's done it our whole life. He'll realize it's a mistake a few months down the road and then he'll have to abandon ship. Do you think I don't know my own family?" he said, raising an eyebrow at Scott.

"Damn. I never knew you were this perceptive."

"When you say you don't want the job, Bennett will step up. He'll see what a disaster it is, then he'll have to figure out how to close it all down. He got himself into this mess. Let him get himself out."

Scott focused on his beer, holding it possessively. "They did this because apparently, I was saying that I wanted to do it. I told Kim that at the funeral."

"When your mother was being laid to rest and you were dealing with all the stress and pressure of a few hundred people flocking around you? Yeah, that sounds like a good time to make life decisions."

"Yeah, but Bennett asked me about it a couple of weeks ago, and I said I was still interested in it."

"Look, I love my mom and I love my brother. But they overstepped here. My mom did it because she truly had good intentions, however skewed, and Bennett is such a mama's boy he'd do anything to please her. You love Felicity. That's what matters. Go get her."

"And just leave them here to flounder with this new organization?"

"Like I said, Bennett will step up. And even if he doesn't, they can hire somebody, a professional—someone who's done this work before. I know you've done the work to some extent, but there are people who specialize in this."

"Yeah, but the whole point is that this way we can make all the changes that my mother wanted. What if somebody else doesn't want to make those changes?"

"Then they do it their way. I don't want to sound disrespectful to your mother, but are you a hundred percent sure the changes she wanted to make were the right ones?"

Scott thought about that.

"I loved your mother like I love my own. But your mother's heart was too big for her chest sometimes. In organizations like this, you need someone who's also got their eye on

the books and is making decisions from a business stand-
point and not just from an emotional one."

As Scott let that settle in, he was shocked with himself
for not having really thought it through before. Scott was a
businessman. He never made emotional decisions at work.
But his mother was an emotional subject for him. He had to
admit that it was possible he had a blind spot when it came
to her.

Lake waved at someone and held up a finger. He
grabbed Scott's shoulder. "Think about it, man. And then go
get her."

Lake walked away, leaving Scott feeling something he
hadn't felt since the moment this problem got dumped in
his lap—hope.

27

I took Scott four hours and fifteen minutes to make it to Indianapolis. He would've left the night before if he hadn't had all those beers. But he'd left the house at six o'clock this morning and made it by ten-thirty Central time, eleven-thirty Indianapolis time.

It was taking everything within him not to text Felicity to tell her he was there. He didn't want her hiding from him. Now he felt like a stalker, but he had to see her so he could let her know...well, he hadn't worked out the exact details of what he'd say, but he'd figure it out.

She had mentioned the grocery store where her mother worked, calling it by name several times. So he found himself with a list of all of the locations of that particular grocery store pulled up on his phone, and here he sat in the parking lot of the first one on the list, making the call. Seven stores in, he had a winner.

He sat in the parking lot of her mother's place of business, wondering what the hell was wrong with him. What was he gonna do, just walk in there and look for someone who looked like Felicity? What if he found her? Would he promise that he was not a stalker or a psycho and ask if she could give up Felicity's location? Would she not want to know why he didn't just text her? And what if she wasn't working today?

He needed to think this through. But delaying at his aunt's party that night had gotten him into this situation. He should've told her right then that he chose her. He'd fucked up royally, and all he could do now was hope against hope that he could make this right.

He couldn't sit there a second longer. He got out of the car and headed up the sidewalk. He took pause when he found two women sitting at a stone table and benches outside looking happy as two birds in a nest. The thing that made him look twice was that it was a cold December Indianapolis day. It had to be thirty-five degrees out there. But the two of them didn't even seem to notice.

The one with reddish blond hair looked up and smiled at him, and he broke stride, taken by a familiarity in her face.

He slowed down, really studying her. She looked at her friend who looked back at her, and then they both set their gaze on him, not unkind, just curious.

He walked over to them. "I'm looking for Rebecca Haley."

The two of them met each other's gaze again and then the brunette looked back at him, this time more seriously. "Can I help you, son?"

Scott rarely felt threatened by women, but he got the idea from this one that she did not suffer fools. "My name is Scott Stover. I'm a friend of Felicity Haley's. I was hoping to find her mother here."

The brunette spoke again. "What kind of friend?"

He realized his opportunity to speak to these women

was finite, and so he said, "The kind who is madly in love with her and desperately hopes to find her so I can convince her to be with me."

This softened both women. They looked at one another bemused, or maybe amused. The redhead pointed at Scott and said, "I think this is him."

The brunette was skeptical. "You sure?"

The redhead pulled out her phone and hunted and pecked into it. The two women stared at the phone, waiting. A moment later, whatever popped up onto the screen satisfied them.

He really hoped they hadn't just warned Felicity. But beggars couldn't be choosers. "Was that her?"

"It was Sebastian," the redhead said, and Scott's heart filled with the joy of knowing that he found the right person and that she had the foresight not to text her daughter. That meant she might be in his corner.

He was so relieved that all he could do was try to explain himself and hope for the best. "The second they approached me with that job, I should've said definitively no, but my mom was really important to me, and I thought I was betraying her to not live out her legacy. But I had this talk with my cousin, and he helped me see that I felt obligated due to my loyalty to her and other things I couldn't give her before she died, and that maybe I had wrapped those ideals up in my grieving process...which I think I'm still going through, even though I always say I grieved her while she was still living and was done with the grieving by the time she died since it was such a relief to not have her suffering any longer. Regardless, I haven't been thinking clearly. I may be a bit off my game."

The brunette chuckled. "Ya think?"

He took a breath to massage his forehead while the two

women had a good chuckle at his expense. Not that he didn't deserve it.

"Sit down, son," the brunette said, and Scott had a seat on the cold stone bench. She narrowed her gaze. "We heard all about you this past week."

He swallowed hard. "Good or not so good?"

The brunette just stared through him with no expression on her face. Part of him wondered if she was ex-military. Maybe she was one of the soldiers who interrogated suspects. Wouldn't surprise him a bit.

The redhead, who he now assumed was Felicity's mom, took the other lady by the wrist in a way that was more romantic and flirty than friendly. "She's messing with you. It was all good."

"Mostly," the brunette said, crossing her arms over her chest, but then slipping in a wink that he would've missed if he would've blinked.

He turned to the redhead. "Are you Ms. Haley?"

"I am, sweetie."

"I'm so sorry for coming up to you like this. But I knew she wouldn't reply to my texts. I just want to see her. Is there any way you would let me know how to find her?"

She knitted her eyebrows together. "Honey, I am so sorry to be the one to tell you this, but you have come here in vain."

His heart sank. He had to get to her. Maybe he could convince her. "Is there any way you'd let me know how to find her?"

"You can find her," the brunette said, "but you've got a hell of a drive ahead of you."

Scott looked between the two women, confused. "Wait, she's not here?"

"I'm so sorry," her mom said. "She and Sebastian left for Florida the other day."

Scott had to orient himself. "She went back to Florida?"

"Yep," the brunette said, looking proud. "No reason for her to stay here anymore." She took Rebecca's hand and squeezed it, the two women exchanging a look that could only be described as love.

He'd been too absorbed in his own situation to really gauge what had been happening here. Felicity's mom was in love with this woman. Felicity was no longer tied to Indianapolis, because this extremely capable, somewhat scary, brunette woman was taking care of her mother. He would hug her, but he didn't want to get his ass kicked.

"Just so I'm clear, she's back there permanently?"

Her mom beamed. "She's giving the catering business a go with her friend Raven. I've told her all along that's what she should do."

Scott slumped, letting it all sink in. Felicity was in Santa Rosa, for good. He didn't have to move to Indianapolis. Not that that would've been the worst thing in the world, but Felicity was in their town, living permanently from what it sounded like. He'd already cleared it with his boss to move to Indianapolis. He'd just change the venue.

He woke up from his reverie, looking between the two women. "I've got to get on a plane."

"What about your car over there?" the brunette asked. "Is that a rental?

"No, it's mine. I drove up from Nashville."

"You're just gonna leave your car behind?"

He looked down at his phone. "I won't make the trip in one day. I'll come back for it."

The brunette looked him up and down. "Moneybags here'll

be back for his car." She gave him a rueful smile, and he realized he was starting to like her. "Before you go, big shot, tell us, who's gonna run that center for domestic abuse survivors if not you?"

He frowned. "I'm not sure. I suggested they list the job, but if I know my cousin and my mom, they'll try to run it themselves."

The two women cut their glances at each other in the exact same way.

Rebecca squinted at him. "What if we had another option available?"

He eyed the two women. "Are the two of you interested in the job?"

"We've been talking about it," the brunette said.

He realized that Felicity had filled them in on the whole story, and they'd been expecting him to come after her. "So you knew I was not going to take the job?"

"We know Felicity is wonderful, and we knew you would have to be a fool not to come after her," Rebecca said.

He remembered Felicity saying that her mom had been abused by her husband. She knew a thing or two about it. There was no better person to help other survivors than a survivor herself. "Are the two of you really interested in this? The foundation's in Nashville."

Felicity's mom set her elbows on the table. "I've been tied to this godforsaken city my whole life. If my daughter isn't here, I have no reason to be here, as long as Judy wants to go."

He looked at Judy. "And you?"

"I'll go wherever she goes."

He scratched his forehead, not believing his luck. "Let me get you in touch with my aunt and my cousin."

The two women smiled at one another. They exchanged

numbers with him, and both women indulged Scott in a hug.

He pointed at each of them. "I'll be seeing a lot more of the two of you."

"We like merlot, if you're wondering what to bring to Easter dinner," Judy said.

He grinned. "Noted. Thank you both."

They sent him on his way, and he headed for the airport.

28

F elicity swept into Gwendolen and Rob's kitchen, dropping off a tray of empty wine glasses. "We better get a move on the champagne. It's almost midnight."

"On it," Raven said, popping a bottle. She poured glasses and Felicity grabbed another bottle. "Wait," Raven said, handing her a small plastic cup with just a few sips of champagne in it. Raven held up her own cup to Felicity. "To my new partner," Raven said, beaming.

Felicity tried to match her smile. She really was thrilled to be in business with Raven, but her heart was hurting from not hearing from Scott since Christmas Day. He had tried to carry on a conversation with her, but she had shut him down. She wasn't ready to engage in small talk. If he wanted her, he needed to come right out with it. None of this pussyfooting around.

Felicity held up a glass. "To our business."

They tapped the cups together and each took a sip before setting them aside and getting back to filling the glasses for the party guests.

"I'm serious, Felicity. When you called, it was like a life raft. Can you imagine me doing this party alone?"

"You would've found somebody."

"I would've made Easton do it and he needs to be at his bar tonight. I'd have been on Chapman and Logan's shit list for months."

"They would've lived."

She could feel Raven side-eyeing her as they both poured. "You doing okay?"

Felicity glanced at her. "What? Am I putting too much in each glass?" Felicity knew what Raven was asking, but she needed a delay tactic.

"I'm just checking on you," Raven said, having Felicity's number.

"It was just a fling. Few weeks of fun."

"Right," Raven said, glancing at her again.

Felicity bumped her with her hip. "I mean it. I'm all good. I'll be back on the scene in no time. Especially now that I'm here permanently."

"Mmm-hmm."

"I mean it. I don't wanna be tied down, anyway. I'm a free spirit. I'd like to date around." It had been the truth a while back. Felicity supposed it had become less true for her in the past year. Since that first weekend with Scott, she hadn't really had any interest in any other man. She hadn't slept with anyone else. It was definitely the most celibate time of her life since she'd turned seventeen.

They loaded trays with glasses. "I'm sorry you can't be with Easton tonight," Felicity said.

Raven shrugged. "I am too, but we've both chosen nighttime careers. We'll spend the day tomorrow ringing in the new year."

Felicity picked up a tray. "Is that what they're calling it

these days?" she waggled her eyebrows and headed out into the crowd.

Both women served all the guests with the glasses of champagne and then met back in the kitchen, where Gwendolen was pouring more glasses.

"Oh please," Raven said. "Let me handle that."

"Don't be ridiculous," Gwendolen said, giving Felicity a wink. Felicity knew a little bit about Gwendolen's background. She had been Rob's housecleaner, but after a weekend on a yacht pretending to be Rob's girlfriend at his request, the two had fallen in love. Felicity had known her a little before the party, but she'd gotten to know her even better over the past few days as they put the finishing touches on this party.

Gwendolen had insisted on helping Felicity with all the decorations. She wasn't the type to sit back and supervise. She was the type to roll up her sleeves and work up a sweat, which was exactly what she'd done alongside Felicity.

"I think we got everyone inside," Felicity said.

"There're a few stragglers by the pool," Gwendolen said, handing Felicity the tray of plastic cups they'd gotten specifically for guests who chose to hang in the pool area.

Felicity took it and made her way toward the pool, Gwendolen following behind her. "I'll get the door for you."

Felicity thought some nice party guest would have opened the door for her, but she wouldn't argue with the lady of the house.

The only group she saw out there was the one containing her own friends. Seanna and Blake, Maya and Bo, Marigold and Dane, and Meade and Ryder congregated in a group near the hot tub. She thought about how lucky each of these couples were to have found one another and fallen for each other the way they had. Each couple had such a unique and special bond, it almost made her teary. She couldn't think of anyone she'd rather ring in the new year with than these people. Well, she could think of one person, but he was in Nashville and she was in Santa Rosa and that was the end of the story.

She approached them, wiping her sentimentality off her face and replacing it with a smile. "Champagne all around?" she asked, holding the tray by her shoulder.

"Yes, please," Seanna said, taking two of the glasses, helping her and Gwendolen pass them around.

"Did we get everyone?" Felicity asked, peering into the group who all seemed to have formed a wall of sorts, boys in the middle girls on the edge.

"Look here," Seanna said, holding up two glasses. "I've ended up with an extra. Here you go," she said, handing Felicity the glass.

"Oh no, I can't. I'm—"

Gwendolen put her hand on Felicity's shoulder. "Oh, but I think you can."

Gwendolen took the cup from Seanna and pressed it into Felicity's hand as the crowd parted to expose Scott standing there, holding a cup of champagne.

She was glad that her tray was empty, because she almost dropped it to the ground. "Scott," she said, her voice coming out in a whisper like she'd seen a ghost. Her body went as cold as if she had seen one.

"Felicity," he said, taking a step toward her.

She looked around and realized Gwendolen was ushering the whole group inside. She turned back toward Felicity with a wink. When Felicity tried to walk toward her, she made a shooing motion and then pointed at Scott with a nod and a thumbs up.

Resigned to her friends' matchmaking, she turned to Scott. "What are you doing?"

"I didn't take the job."

Her heart pounded in her chest as she lifted her chin. "That's a shame. It's what your mother would've wanted, right?"

"I loved my mother more than anyone on earth, and I want to honor her now and until the day I die. But that doesn't mean I have to take on her life's work."

She considered him, keeping her wall firmly intact. "Well, good for you."

She turned to walk away and he grabbed her arm. "Wait."

She let her shoulders sag. "What is it, Scott?"

"I want to move here."

She looked him up and down. "It's a free country."

He put his cup down and took her by the arms, running his hands over her shoulders and then back down to her biceps. "I want to move here with you."

"I'm already here."

"Then I want to be here with you."

She narrowed her gaze. "How do I know I'm not just another project you've run headlong into and want to complete? How do I know you won't take your mobile job and be right back to Nashville before Easter?"

"Well, it's looking like I will be there, with you visiting your mom and Judy."

Felicity blinked. "When did you talk to my mom and Judy?"

"This morning when I drove into Indianapolis and found her."

Felicity set her drink and the tray down. "Where did you find her?"

"At the grocery store."

"How did you..."

"You mentioned it a few times, so I went down the list, calling each one."

"Is there some reason you didn't just call me?"

"You don't have a history of taking my phone calls once we are separated by a state or two."

She let out a harumph, shaking her head at him. "You were in Indy this morning?"

"Yep."

"What'd you do, get a plane down here?"

"Yeah, but flights were a little difficult, so I've been sort of all around the southeast, but that's another story." He took her hands. "What matters is I'm here. And I'm not ever leaving you again."

She chewed on her lip. "I don't know, I—"

He shut her up with a kiss, and her knees almost buckled from the sweet familiarity. Her hand went to the back of his head like a honing device, and then she pulled it away, wrenching herself from him. "Scott, I just don't know if I'm—"

"I love you," he said.

Her heart practically melted. "What?" she asked, unable to help herself.

He held onto her shoulders. "I love you. I want to be with you. I don't care if that means we get nearby apartments or if we move into the same one. Hell, we could buy a house together if you want. All I care about is not being away from you a day longer. I spent the last year trying to somehow recreate the spark I had with you a year and some change ago. But it's been you since that day you walked into that coffee shop. It was like I was assigned to you."

She could not help her smile. "Like homework?"

"Like fate."

She rolled her eyes. "I know you did not just say—" He shut her up with another kiss, and she fell into it before pulling away, pointing at him. "You cannot kiss me every time you want me to not talk."

He kissed her again, but this time, she didn't argue.

He pulled away, grinning at her. "I love you like snowflakes love mountaintops."

She cocked her head to the side.

"I love you like fish love water. I love you like sand loves to get in every crack and crevice of your body after a day at the beach."

She started to walk away. "I'm getting out of here." He snatched her back to him and she let him press her against his chest. "I love you like a man who has landed the most special, beautiful, unique, loving, gorgeous-on-the-inside-and-out creature that he's ever met in his life. I love you, Felicity Haley. And I want to start my life with you right now."

She considered him, but there was nothing left to decide.

She was vaguely aware of a group countdown resonating from inside the house. She grabbed handfuls of his shirt, pulling him flush to her. "I love you too, you goofy bastard."

Shouts boomed from inside the house as fireworks exploded in the sky, illuminating it with color. They met each other's gaze once again and went back in for another kiss, Felicity knowing she'd finally made it home.

EPILOGUE

Felicity and Scott sat on a beach blanket watching all of their friends mill around the shore. Cassidy had invited the whole gang who was on the group thread over for a pre-season drink, citing that it would be the last weekend before the official start of the spring break. When every single person in their group showed up, they had to move the party down to the beach.

Seanna and Sebastian approached them. "I'm pretty sure I've never seen this whole group together at once," Seanna said.

"I don't think it's ever happened." Sebastian looked around. "Where's Ashe? We need to get a picture or something. He does this for a living."

"He disappeared a little while ago. Maybe he had the same idea and went for his camera," Seanna said.

"I'll take one of all of you," Scott said.

"You need to be *in* the picture, silly," Sebastian said.

Scott shrugged, but his grin told Felicity he was thrilled to be a part of the group.

They were a pretty amazing group, especially the

women. Seanna was one of the most welcoming and down-to-earth people Felicity had ever met. Maya, while Felicity's polar opposite, was that friend that kept everything under control so you didn't have to worry about a thing. Shayla, who was one of the most beautiful women on earth but couldn't care less, reminded Felicity to always stay humble. Marigold was the only woman in the group more up for anything than Felicity herself.

Desiree brought creativity and a free spiritedness about her that silently encouraged those around her to loosen up and follow their dreams. Cassidy, a little older and wiser than the rest of them and the most giving of her time, kept Felicity doing things like organizing Christmas carol events. Meade, who had rapidly become Felicity's closest friend in the group, was the most like her, but with more brilliance than Felicity contained in her pinky, though she never made anyone feel lesser. Gwendolen helped Felicity see that she should always be true to herself and others, even if you found yourself with more money than God. Felicity loved each of these wonderful women and felt honored to call them her friends and family.

"Don't you think?" Sebastian asked.

Felicity woke up from her reverie. "Hmm?"

Sebastian and Seanna giggled conspiratorially and locked arms, running off to go cause more trouble somewhere. Luckily, their significant others caught each of them before they could do much else, and the two of them split off. Seanna fell into Blake's arms while Sebastian planted a huge kiss on Flynn's lips.

"He was playing with you," Scott said. "We could tell you were daydreaming."

Felicity smiled at their friends. "I've never had a group like this."

"What about Sebastian and Maya?"

"True, but it was just the three of us. There're how many of us here?" Felicity couldn't even count all the friends around her, gathering, laughing, having thoughtful conversations. She'd been on the periphery of this group, only having been around them that week she visited Sebastian a year and a half ago, the weekend of the wedding three months later, and now these past several months, but she'd grown closer with the members of this group in the short time she'd known them than with anybody she'd tried to forge friendships with in the years leading up to now.

"Look at Bo and Maya," Scott said. "I haven't seen her this happy since I first met her."

"They had a teenage girl pick their profile on the adoption website this week. They met with her over Zoom today and said it went really well."

"I'll keep my fingers crossed for them," Scott said.

"If that doesn't work out, something else will. And I don't say that because of fate. I say it because Maya will make it happen. She's a doer."

"I believe it." Scott checked his phone, and Felicity raised a curious eyebrow. "It's Judy."

"Work stuff?" Felicity asked. As it turned out, Scott was able to help with the shelter remotely. He handled the financials and budgets...general CFO stuff. He told Felicity it was fairly simple, and he needed to fill his nights away from her anyway. Spending time together was one of their challenges because of their alternate schedules, but they were figuring it out.

"Nah. Just a funny meme."

Felicity grinned. "Who knew your new best friend would be a middle-aged lesbian."

He shrugged. "We get one another. She still calls me moneybags."

"I like that nickname."

"It definitely confuses people, because I'm not rolling in it like Rob. And conversely, I'm not broke where it would work for irony."

"That's why I like it. Keeps people guessing."

"True," he said, shrugging concession and then pulling her in close to him, kissing her forehead.

Felicity considered their group. "It feels like everyone is settled...like everyone's paired up and solid in their careers or getting there. Is that what happens when you get in your thirties? Everything falls into place?"

"I think things start to come into focus."

"Do you think we'll all get bored now that we're all settled?" Felicity asked with a smile, knowing she was content as could be.

"I think new adventures await us every day. Besides, you and I can live vicariously through Lake. He's always got something to keep the conversation interesting."

Felicity thought about all of Scott's yummy cousins, knowing they would each continue to pique their interest.

Scott pointed. "Look, Ashe did go get his camera. He's got a tripod. Damn expensive-looking one at that."

"I'm sure it's some kind of special device made to withstand the elements like the beach and the wind."

"All right, people," Ashe shouted. "Everyone gather. We're taking a picture."

Felicity hauled herself up, and she and Scott headed to the group and let Ashe get them in place.

"Where are you going to stand?" Ashe's husband, Ethan, asked.

"Don't you worry about me, sweetie. I know I usually

take the pictures, but it's too rare an occasion when all your favorite people are in one place. I've got me a spot." He looked through the lens one more time. "All right, we've got ten seconds." He rushed over, getting in place.

"Everybody say Seaside," Cassidy's husband, Jesse, said.

"Everyone say South Walton," shouted Tobias, Desiree's permanently on-again boyfriend, referencing the name used to encompass the entire area of communities where they lived.

"Everybody say 30A," Seanna shouted.

And that was the one they landed on, all of them shouting the name of the highway that contained all of the beautiful communities where they resided in this little place of beach gold in the panhandle of Florida. And with a click of the camera, all of their stories were in the books.

FROM THE AUTHOR

It feels like the end of an era! I've been writing the Love Along Hwy 30A series since 2011! Most of that time was spent writing and rewriting Seaside Sweets, trying to get it right. You could say I learned to write on that book. It went through I can't even tell you how many critique groups and contests and helpful people giving feedback. But in the end, I'm really glad I stayed the course and never gave up on these characters.

How could I? They have become a part of me. I feel like they're my friends and family. I know seven books is an odd amount, but that was exactly how many I needed to make sure everyone got their story told. I truly love each and every one of their flawed personalities, and I can guarantee you there is a small part of me in every one of them (some a little more than others!). Though one of the best parts about writing characters is to "be" someone you aren't for a moment in time, which is a true treasure.

I will love every series I write (and if I don't, I will stop writing it), but this one will always hold a special place in my heart.

The Teague brothers will carry this torch through the next series. I'll keep you posted on their debut through my newsletter (sign up at melissachambers.com). In the meantime, you can peek in on the Destiny Dunes gang who work right down the street in Destin, Florida. But let me tell you, they're a hot mess!

Thank you, reader, for sticking this series out with me! I can't begin to tell you how much you make my day with your engagement in my Facebook reader group (Books, Beaches, and Bellinis), responding to my newsletters, or reaching out to me on some social media. I'm giving you my heart with each book, and to have you use your reading time to read my words makes me so humble and appreciative.

Happy beach reading to you and yours!

ALSO BY MELISSA CHAMBERS

Love Along Hwy 30A Series:

Seaside Sweets: A Steamy Small Town Beach Read

Seacrest Sunsets: A Steamy Opposites-Attract Beach Read

Seagrove Secrets-A Steamy Brother's Best Friend Beach Read

WaterColor Wishes: A Steamy Enemies-to-Lovers Romance

Grayton Beach Dreams: A Steamy May-December Romance

Rosemary Beach Kisses: A Steamy Single Dad Romance

Christmas in Santa Rosa: A Steamy Second Chance Romance

The Destiny Dunes Series:

Down for Her: A Riches-to-Rags Steamy Romance

Up for Seconds: A Second Chance Steamy Romance

Coming Around: A Friends-to-Lovers Steamy Romance

In His Heart: A Harbored Secrets Steamy Romance

Over the Moon: A Forced Proximity Steamy Romance

Under the Stars: An Enemies to Lovers Steamy Romance

Young Adult titles:

The Summer Before Forever (Before Forever #1)

Falling for Forever (Before Forever #2)

Courting Carlyn (Standalone)

Two Boy Summer (Standalone)

ABOUT THE AUTHOR

Melissa Chambers writes contemporary novels for young, new, and actual adults. A Nashville native, she spends her days working in the music industry and her nights getting lost in her characters. While she's slightly obsessed with alt rock, she leaves the guitar playing to her husband and kid. She never misses a chance to play a tennis match, listen to an audiobook, or eat a bowl of ice cream. (Rocky road, please!) She's a member of several online and local writers groups, all of which she treasures and is unendingly grateful for, and has served as president for the Music City Romance Writers. She is the author of the Love Along Hwy 30A series, the Destiny Dunes series, the Before Forever series (YA), Courting Carlyn (YA), and Two Boy Summer (YA).

BB bookbub.com/profile/melissa-chambers

a amazon.com/Melissa-Chambers/e/B00MRU380K

f facebook.com/MelissaChambersAuthor

O instagram.com/melissachambersauthor

Made in the USA
Middletown, DE
05 October 2022

12035876R00146